Maybe you accidentally called your teacher "Mom" in front of the whole class.

Maybe you missed the **tie-breaking** goal
in your **championship game.**

Maybe your internet cut out just **milliseconds**
before you were about to **obliterate** your archenemy
during an online gaming marathon.

Well, can I just tell you something?

THAT wasn't a bad week!

THIS IS A BAD WEEK!!

IN FACT IT'S THE...

WORST WEEK
EVER!

I'm at a new school
with the meanest **bully**
in the universe.

Don't be fooled
by the School
Captain badge

My mom has just
married a **vampire**.
Seriously!

Step-Dracula.
Yikes!

Fruitcake.
Double yikes

My dad is driving
a giant **toilet** on
wheels. Literally!

Mary Poopins
or the Whizz
Wizard. He can't
decide.

I'm pretty sure my
cat has been **kidnapped**
by **ALIENS**.

Where are
you, Captain
Fluffykins?

And right now, I've got a major case of food poisoning, **PLUS** I'm hanging off the edge of a **thirty-foot-high** diving tower in front of my **entire** class, wearing nothing but rapidly **disappearing** crocheted swimming trunks.

AND IT'S ONLY...

Text and illustrations copyright © 2024 by Eva Amores and Matt Cosgrove

All rights reserved. Published by Scholastic Inc., *Publishers since 1920.* SCHOLASTIC and associated logos are trademarks and/or registered trademarks of Scholastic Inc. This edition published under license from Scholastic Australia Pty Limited. First published by Scholastic Australia Pty Limited in 2022.

The publisher does not have any control over and does not assume any responsibility for author or third-party websites or their content.

ISBN 978-1-338-85754-2

10 9 8 7 6 5 4 3 2 1   24 25 26 27 28

Printed in the U.S.A.   132

First U.S. printing 2024

EVA AMORES & MATT COSGROVE

MONDAY

Scholastic Inc.

AND IT ALL STARTS HERE!

5:00 a.m.

"WAKE UP!"

TV moms wake up their kids with a loving kiss on the forehead. A delicate, gentle shake. A soft, singsong whisper of "time to rise and shine."

My mom is **NOT** a TV mom.

"WAKE UP!"

She is standing in my bedroom doorway, flicking the light switch on and off. Like this...

CLICK!

Each burst of light stabs at my eyes. I try to pull my covers over my face, but they are whipped off my body.

"Up. **Now!** We're leaving in twenty minutes, **Justin Chase.**"

That's me. **Justin Chase.** Not the international pop star Justin Chase. It's pretty easy to tell us apart!

JUSTIN CHASE
Me, a regular kid

O followers
(Not allowed on
social media)

$5 haircut from
Mr. Snipzy

Scar from
Mr. Snipzy
cutting my ear

Twelve years old—
could pass for ten

My mom says
I'm handsome
(but she just
married a vampire
so her taste is
questionable)

Mosquito
bite

Totally
empty

Awesome elbow
scab from when
I tripped
the other day

Unlimited
supply of belly
button lint

Hand-me-down jeans
from my cousin Barry
(hole in the knee by
me—not on purpose)

Crickets

Allergy alert
bracelet
(gold-plated)

Shoes from that weir
middle aisle in ALDI

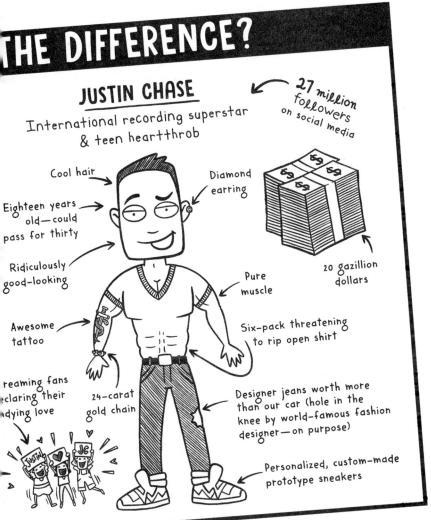

JUSTIN CHASE

International recording superstar & teen heartthrob

27 million followers on social media

Cool hair

Diamond earring

Eighteen years old—could pass for thirty

Ridiculously good-looking

Awesome tattoo

Pure muscle

20 gazillion dollars

Six-pack threatening to rip open shirt

reaming fans claring their dying love

24-carat gold chain

Designer jeans worth more than our car (hole in the knee by world-famous fashion designer—on purpose)

Personalized, custom-made prototype sneakers

Um, yeah. So basically all we have in common is our name. And for me, it's a **CURSE!**

"Hurry up! We're leaving in ten minutes!"

That's my mom. She's tiny, but don't be fooled. Do NOT mess with this lady. Repeat:

DO NOT MESS WITH THIS LADY!

Her name is Angelica Mary-Grace Joy Manalo Dela-Cruz, but everyone calls her **Angel.** Except me. I call her **"YES, MOM!"**

She's a registered nurse.

She speaks three languages.

She runs marathons.

She knows martial arts.

She's NEVER late.

DO NOT MESS WITH HER.

Also, she gives **great hugs!**

Just not right at this exact moment in time.

"MOVE IT, MISTER!"

Other important Mom inf

LIKES	DISLIKES
• Rules	• Rule breaking
• Cat videos	• Rule breakers
	• Rule bending
	• Rule ignoring
	• Rule forgetting
	• Rule flouting
	• Rule questioning
	• Frogs

hen IT begins.

"TEN SECONDS! TEN, NINE..."

My mom **loves** a countdown.

he should work at NASA! →

MOM'S DREAM JOB

I congratulate myself for already being fully dressed.

leeping in my clothes was a stroke of genius!

"EIGHT, SEVEN..."

I grab my pre-packed overnight bag. This is the

ew me: organized, efficient, responsible.

"SIX, FIVE..."

Ready to rule my new life. New home. New school.

ew me. It's going to be **the best week** EVER! I can feel

in my guts.

"FOUR, THREE, TWO..."

Everything I own is crammed into cardboard

oxes, ready to be moved to my dad's place later

oday. Goodbye, old room, old life.

Before Mom can say **"One,"**

race past her, down the hallway,

nd out the front door.

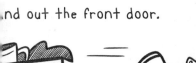

I don't know what happens if she ever gets to "**ONE**." And I don't plan on finding out.

HOOOOOOOONNNNK!

That's the car horn in case you idn't hear it, though I'm pretty ure they heard it on the **moon!** ➤

Hey! Keep it down!

HOOOOOOOOONNNNNK!

Dogs are **HOWLING.** Lights in the neighboring houses are flicking on.

The guy holding his hand down on the horn, sitting straight upright in the front seat while **glaring** coldly at me out the window with his lifeless, beady eyes, is my brand-new **stepdad.**

And I mean **BRAND-NEW.** My mom just married him last night.

Here are the **highlights** from the wedding:

What happen to oldies at weddings?!

Uncle Ray attempting the Worm
(and then giving me ten bucks
to help him up off the dance floor)

Aunty Beryl doing the Funky Chicken
(and then giving me ten bucks
for fetching her asthma inhaler)

Also good: the all-you-can-
eat buffet. I did my best!

Here are the **lowlights**:

The "cake"

How can cake be a lowlight?
Because it was FRUITCAKE! Fruit
does not belong in cake!! What a
SCAM! At least the icing was OK.

Having to wear this stupid suit and
then smile for ten million photos

Photograph number
9,876,432!

I throw my bag into the trunk, **SLAM** it shut, and then jump in the back seat. My cat is already buckled up in the seat next to me in his "Pawtable Kitty Kat Karrier," giving me the **EVIL EYE**.

He is **THE** most miserable cat on the planet, but he's **my** cat and I love him. This love is **NOT** returned in any way WHATSOEVER. I suspect it's because of his name: **CAPTAIN FLUFFYKINS.**

I honestly don't know what I was thinking. In my defense, I was five when I named him and he **USED** to be **CUTE**.

THEN:

Other Captain Fluffykins facts:

LIKES
- Sleeping
- Scratching the couch
- Scratching the curtains
- Death-staring
- Scratching the doors
- Scratching me

DISLIKES
- Everybody
- Everything
- Scratching his scratching post

&
NOW:

5:50 a.m.

We've been driving for half an hour now and for half an hour my mom has been twisted around in the front passenger seat looking back at me, rattling off a **NEVER-ENDING** list of rules.

"Do your homework as soon as you get home. Check your answers **twice**. Do **ALL** of the extra credit. Be polite to all of the teachers. Make eye contact. Speak clearly. Use your manners. Say good morning to the principal. Always say please and thank you. Smile. Make good friends. Stay away from **TROUBLEMAKERS**. Don't talk in class. Pay attention. Raise your hand. Answer questions. Comb your hair. Stand up **straight**. Polish your shoes. Make sure your shirt is tucked in. Make sure you pack everything you need in your schoolbag. Take your EpiPen with you **everywhere**. **ALWAYS** check the ingredients label before you eat anything. Wear a hat if you go outside. Take a jacket in case it gets cold. Write neatly. Take pride in all of your work. Do not even think about picking your nose. Don't even touch the edge of your nostril. Hands stay entirely away from your nose. Sneeze into your elbow. **Always** have an extra handkerchief in your pocket. Wash your hands — for twenty seconds — after you blow your nose. Wash your hands after you go to the bathroom. Wash your hands before you eat. Wash your hands after you eat. Wash your hands if you touch anything. Wash your hands if you haven't washed your hands in a while. **Wash your hands.** Eat your greens. No junk food. Brush your teeth for two minutes — use the timer! No video games on a weeknight. Only one hour of video games on Saturday and Sunday. I **WILL** find out if you play for longer. Do some form of exercise — **every day**. Be good to your sweet Nan — you're lucky to have her. Help with the housework. Make your bed — **properly**. Take out the trash. Wash your hands. Don't forget to feed Captain Fluffykins. Listen to your father, unless what he is saying contradicts what I have told you, then listen to **ME**. I will be the voice in your head. Wash your hands. Always do the right thing. Pull up your socks. I will call you every day. You **WILL** pick up. Message me if anything bad happens. Message me if anything good happens. Just message me. **Anytime**. But no games on the phone. It is for emergencies only. In bed by 8:00 p.m. every night. Lights out by 8:30 p.m. You need your rest. No watching YouTube. No watching anything that is rated over PG. You are only allowed online for homework assignments. Do not talk to any strangers on the internet. Do not talk to any strangers on the street. Only cross the road at dedicated pedestrian crosswalks. Look both ways **TWICE** before crossing the road, even if you have the walking signal. Remember what happened to your poor cousin Ric. Tie your shoelaces properly. Don't pee on the toilet seat. Clean up after yourself. Wash behind your ears. Make sure your fingernails are clean. Don't forget to floss. Do not let your room get too messy. Do not let the dog sleep in your room. Do not whine. Be happy. Be a good boy!

"Yes, Mom," I repeat each time she pauses for breath, although I stopped listening a while ago. I'm staring straight ahead at the back of my stepdad's head. Did I mention he's a **VAMPIRE?** Well, he is.

SPOT THE DIFFERENCE*

*There is NONE. Practically twins!

DRACULA

OK, so I'm still working on this list, but trust me. He's a vampire!

IRREFUTABLE proof my new stepdad is a vampire:

- His name is Vlad
- Pasty, pale skin
- Avoids sunlight
- Only wears black
- Works night shift at the hospital blood bank (where he met Mom)
- Unlimited access to blood!!
- Likes to count (not as much as Mom though)
- .
- .
- .

It looks **spooky** and it is most likely, definitely **haunted,** but it is massive and I get the entire upstairs attic as my bedroom. **SWEET!**

It's practically a **MANSION,** but my dad could afford it because it was sold super cheap. It was for sale for ages and no one was interested. Probably because it's **HAUNTED.** And also because it backs on to **the Cemetery for Elite Athletes,** which is oddly specific and very weird, but my dad **LOVES** a bargain!

That's my Nan. NOT a ghost!

RENOVATOR'S DELIGHT
~~CEA~~SED ESTATE

SOLD!
We can't believe it, either!

SPIRITED COMMUN...
HAUNTING ORIGINAL
ARCHITECTURAL FEATURES
CONVENIENTLY LOCATED NEAR
THE DEAD CENTER OF TOWN

13

Lucky I'm not superstitious!

SO HERE'S THE DEAL: I'm going to be based at Dad's house from now on.

Since Mom married Step-Dracula (last night)...

Photograph Number 3,456,138

"we" (i.e., Mom and Dad) all decided at a Family Meeting (boring)...

she is moving into his place (fancy apartment in the city)...

DON'T BREAK ANYTHING! DON'T BREAK ANYTHING! DON'T BREAK ANYTHING!

and since they both mostly work night shifts (because she's a nurse and he's a vampire)...

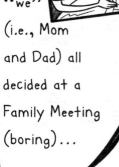

that I would move in with Dad (and Nan) during the week (because he's awake during daylight hours —mostly—PLUS his new place is massive)...

and spend weekends with Mom (after she gets back from her tropical island honeymoon)...

which is why they are rushing to get me out of the car because they need to get to the airport and Mom is NEVER late.

DO YOU FOLLOW?

Dad has sauntered out of the house and down the driveway to greet us. He always looks like he's moving in slow motion, as though he's wading through mud. He is **NEVER** in a hurry. It drives Mom "up the wall!"

He's casually scratching his armpit. But some part of Dad's body is always itching, so it could be worse! **MUCH WORSE.**

And he's just wearing his boxer shorts and UGG boots. That's almost **overdressed** by Dad's standards.

Dad at the beach

Dad mowing the lawn

Dad watching TV

I leap out of the car and Dad grins. "The big guy is here—the **Juz Man!**" Despite being the man who named me "Justin," Dad never uses my **actual** name.

Names my Dad calls me INSTEAD of Justin:

- Juzmeister
- JuJu ChooChoo
- Sir Jousting Chasealot
- Justin Time for Dinner
- The Justinator
- Judge Choozy
- Justin Case I Forget
- Dustin Justin
- J-Dawg
- Juzzo
- Juzza
- Justo
- Super J
- JuzJuz
- Juicy C
- Emperor Justinus
- Big J
- Little J
- Justifizzle
- Jay Cee
- Dr. Jay

continues...

"Give me five, J to the C!"

Gets me **EVERY TIME!**

Stepdad rises out of the front car seat like a, well, like a vampire out of a coffin. He stands and faces Dad and it is basically every **wildlife documentary** you've ever seen, where the two big male animals in the group face off against each other.

VLADAMIR.

HAROLD.

GRUNCH!

CRACK!

No one calls Stepdad "Vladimir." It's just Vlad.

No one calls Dad "Harold." It's always Harry.

Mom breaks the **AWKWARD** handshake. "You'll catch a cold out here in your **underwear**, Harry! Here's the cat. Here's the leftover wedding cake. **ENJOY!** Justin's boxes should be delivered later this afternoon. We need to get going or we'll be **LATE**. Call me if **anything** happens!"

Then Mom turns to me and gentle smile lifts the corners f her mouth. Her eyes are **listening** as she envelops me n one of her full-body hugs hat transfer warmth, **LOVE**, eace, and tenderness but also RESTRICT BREATHING.

"I love you more than nything," she says softly.

"**More** than cat videos?" I check (it's our thing).

"**MORE** than cat videos," she confirms and kisses me epeatedly on each cheek, my forehead, and the top of my head efore I **wriggle** out of her arms.

And then the smile evaporates. "Follow the **RULES!** Be **good**. Have fun, but **NOT** too much fun. Message me. Call me. I'll be back soon."

Then she's in the car with Stepdad driving off to the airport. Their tropical island awaits. I wave goodbye and blow kisses. (To Mom, not Stepdad.)

I walk in through the front door and I'm **KNOCKED** over.
Flat on my back. Standing on my chest, licking my face like it's
a melting ice cream cone in summer, is NICKERS, Dad's dog.

"**ERRRRRGGGGGGGGGHHHHHHHHHHHH!** Get off
me, Nickers!" I cry, unsuccessfully trying to push the dog
away from my face. Her tail is wagging like full-speed windshield
wipers and her barks of happiness echo through the house.

Not sure what breed of dog she is.

Dad laughs his roaring belly laugh, his tummy actually
JIGGLING as he enters the foyer. Captain Fluffykins hisses
angrily through his little window. Nickers is Captain Fluffykins's
lifelong sworn **ENEMY!** I'm not sure how it is going to work
with them together under the same roof again.

So we meet again! You slobbering, butt-sniffing buffoon.

**Woof Woof Woof Woof

"Settle down, Nickers!" Dad commands and Nickers obeys. She **mostly** does whatever Dad says, ever since the day he brought her home from the **Dog Rescue Center**. She really is a good dog, except for one small character flaw. She has a tendency to **STEAL** things. Anything. Anytime. She's basically a raging **KLEPTOMANIAC**. That's why she's called **Nickers**. Because she **NICKS** everything!

SOME THINGS NICKERS HAS STOLEN THROUGHOUT HISTORY

| My homework (and of course no one believed me) | Dad's car keys AND sunglasses | Nan's undies (they're so big!) | Captain Fluffykins's lunch |

"Best friends, reunited!" Dad proclaims and (rather unwisely I must say) lets Captain Fluffykins out of his portable prison.

You're probably thinking this is where the dog starts chasing the cat.

Well, you don't know Captain Fluffykins.

Nickers runs, YELPING for her life!

IT STARTS HERE!

Nan's room

#@&*!!

Foyer

Not to scale!

HISS!

YELP!

IT ENDS HERE.

A standoff between dog and cat. Nickers is **cornered**. Captain Fluffykins is ready to **POUNCE** on his pooch prey.

33

"Captain Fluffykins! **STOP!**" I shout, panting and out of breath. But that cat has **never** listened to me and clearly isn't about to start listening now.

   He launches himself in a **flying leap** toward Nickers. In a move no one (especially Captain Fluffykins!) sees coming, Nickers ducks down flat on her belly. And my cat, trapped by the laws of physics in his ill-advised **TRAJECTORY**, sails **over** the top of his nemesis and flies straight out the back window, **disappearing** into the murky darkness of the breaking dawn.

In disbelief, I run to the window and scan outside for Captain Fluffykins. I heave a sigh of **relief** when I spot him. He's perched on the ridge of the roof below, like a surly, furry **GARGOYLE**.

GARGOYLE (moderately scary)

CAPTAIN FLUFFYKINS (absolutely terrifying)

"Captain Fluffykins! DON'T MOVE!" I yell. He looks directly at me and gives me his most withering, contempt-filled **death stare**. Suddenly, there's a blinding **FLASH** of light from above.

Captain Fluffykins is **GONE!** Completely **vanished** into thin air.

Dad has finally made it up the stairs. He surveys the room. "Where's the Captain?" he asks jovially.

I turn from the window in **SHOCK** and stammer the only possible explanation. "I think...he's been **abducted**... by **ALIENS**, Dad."

I see my words register in Dad's head and concern washes over his face. He steps toward me, arms outstretched, and he **hugs** me while looking over my head out the window.

"Juzzle Chuzzle, kiddo, I don't think Captain Fluffykins was abducted by aliens. That doesn't make any sense at all... **Firstly**, alien abductions **typically** occur between 1:00 a.m. and 2:00 a.m. It's a fact.

"**Secondly**, there's no way an extraterrestrial expedition to Earth would be wasting their time abducting a **CAT** when I am right here—the **PRIME EXAMPLE** of th male human species of this planet."

I stare at Dad in silence. I shouldn't be too surprised by his response, though. My Dad spends **WAY** too much time on the internet. Every week he's spouting a new **RIDICULOUS** conspiracy theory he's discovered online.

Dad takes my **stunned** silence as acceptance of his logic. "The Captain will turn up, Juzzo. When he's hungry enough, he'll be back. Speaking of food, I reckon it's **breakfast** time."

I turn back to the window and look up to the sky that's slowly filling with the first light of morning. I think I see a star **SPARKLE** in the distance, but Dad is already ushering me down the stairs.

As I walk down to the kitchen, I start to doubt what I saw out the window. It does seem **highly unlikely** that my cat has been abducted by aliens. That kind of **far-fetched, OUTLANDISH** thing only really happens in **PREPOSTEROUS** kids' books.

I convince myself that Captain Fluffykins, wherever he might be, is totally **FINE**. Cats do have nine lives, after all, and I'm pretty sure Captain Fluffykins has only used six of his.

THE CATASTROPHIC CLOSE CALLS OF CAPTAIN FLUFFYKINS

LIFE 1 — The fishbowl

LIFE 2 — The full flush

LIFE 3 — The close shave

LIFE 4 — The freezer

LIFE 5 — The birthday cake

LIFE 6 — The yarn ball

So it's time to focus on more pressing issues, like **BREAKFAST**. I've been awake for one and a half hours and haven't eaten a single thing, and last night's **all-you-can-eat** wedding buffet is just a distant memory. I think I actually hear my stomach **grumbling**. Lucky for me, Dad's fridge is always a **GOLD MINE**.

I open the fridge door expecting to find **this**...

Juice

BACON!

Soft drink

Whipped cream

Leftover pizza

Stinky cheese

Leftover Thai takeout

Leftover Chinese takeout

BBQ chicken

Chocolate cookies

Lone withered carrot

Milk (expired two days ago)

Chocolate milk

Air

X-RAY VIEW
Ice cream

Instead, I find this **BETRAYAL**...

COLOR BY NUMBER
1 = GREEN
2 = GREEN
3 = GREEN
4 = GREEN

X-RAY VIEW
Frozen peas

"What the actual WHAT?! Dad? **EXPLAIN!**" I shriek.

Dad moseys over to the fridge door, smiling. "Pretty impressive, eh, Justarama? I found this new diet on the internet. All the Hollywood **celebrities** are doing it. We only eat **GREEN** food now. Well, as of today. I threw out all the other colored food yesterday. I've committed to this."

"You should **be** committed," I mumble.

Dad is always starting the latest diet he's discovered online. Told you he spends too much time on the internet. It's a **DANGEROUS** place!) Luckily, the diets usually only last a day r two before Dad comes to his senses. Or, more accurately, racks from **hunger**, excessive **FLATULENCE**, or both.

DAD'S PAST DIET DISASTERS

Onion Soup Diet
aka The Tear Gasser

**Omelette
Only Diet**
aka The Rotten Egger

Baked Bean Diet
aka The Wind
Machine

"Someone looks like they could se a kale, cucumber, and cabbage **SENSATION** cleansing **SMOOTHIE**, Justalicious. I'll **whip** one up for you now!" Dad chops up a bunch of green vegetables, puts them into the blender, and hits the button.

WHRROOOAAR!

"What's with all the **kerfuffle?!**" That's Nan. Well, technically she's my dad's Nan. So she's old. **REALLY** old. Not **dinosaur** old, but at least invention-of-the-wheel old. In fact she probably **crocheted** the first wheel.

She can crochet **ANYTHING**. And she does. The usual stuff:

| Teapot cosies | Striped scarves | TP roll dollies | Coat hanger covers | Doilies (What even are doilies?!) |

And the more **experimental**, less successful stuff:

Shower curtain   Umbrella   A hat for Captain Fluffykins

Why I Like hanging out with Nan:

- She tells funny stories about Dad getting in trouble as a boy.
- She swears!
- She taught me how to crochet and we're making a rug together.

> When your dad was a whippersnapper, he gave himself a haircut with the whipper snipper!

BA HA HA!

My Nan is pretty **cool** to be around, so I'm happy to see her as she shuffles into the kitchen.

She repeats, "What's with all the **KERFUFFLE?!**" Nan can't hear very well and she assumes no one else can either, so she repeats things **ALL** the time.

She gives me a great big hug. "Justin, look at **YOU!** We better put a brick on your head to stop you growing. Or am I **shrinking?**"

Feeling pretty HUGGED OUT right now

43

As Nan makes her first of a million cups of tea for the day, Dad presents me with a **bubbling** glass full of green SLOP, which could easily be mistaken for **TOXIC WASTE**.

SPOT THE DIFFERENCE

DAD'S SMOOTHIE   TOXIC WAS

*There is NONE.

Think I rather drink TH

"Get that into ya, Jus Chuz!" He looks at me expectantly, the way Nickers looks at you when

she wants you to scratch her belly.

I sigh and cautiously take a sip. It's **WORSE** than expected! It **GLUGS** into my mouth and I force the **sludge** down my throat, which is doing its best to send the GLOOP straight back up.

"Good stuff, eh, Juzzle?" Dad is beaming with pride. As he watches on, smiling, I gulp down the whole glass of green **GUNK** to get it over with as fast as possible.

"It was **THAT** good? I'll make you **another** one, umbo Chumbo!" Dad turns back to the cutting board.

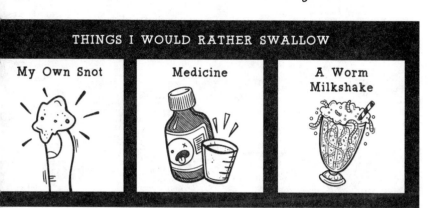

THINGS I WOULD RATHER SWALLOW

My Own Snot

Medicine

A Worm Milkshake

"**I'M FULL! I'M FULL!** No more, thanks, Dad! I better start getting ready for my first day at the **new** school! Want to make a **GOOD IMPRESSION**. Lots to do!" And I bolt out of the kitchen before Dad has a chance to prepare me another cup of **SLIME**.

As I pick up my overnight bag in the foyer, I notice the freezer bag of wedding cake. I decide a bit of icing might be **just the thing** to get rid of the **DISGUSTING** taste in my mouth. I bound up the stairs with both bags and enter my room.

SQUEAK!

Now that I'm not chasing a cat chasing a dog, I can fully appreciate my new bedroom in the breaking daylight.

How I **imagined** my new bedroom...

(Mom doesn't actually let me play the video game, but it is THE most popular game that EVERYONE else on the planet EXCEPT me plays.)

What my new bedroom **actually** looks like...

CLOPPY was my favorite. (Way cooler than Floppy and Sloppy.)

Admittedly, best concert of my life. (Also, ONLY concert of my life.)

"WHAT HAS MY DAD DONE?!"

As explanation: The Hoppy Doppys was my favorite show—when I was **FIVE!**

But something, maybe five-year-old Justin, **COMPELS** me to hit play on **The Hoppy Doppys** CD player. (Where did Dad even find a CD player?!)

"If You're Hoppy and You Know It" blasts out. It **IS** a classic, and before I know it I'm **dancing** around my room with stuffed Cloppy Doppy, doing all the actions and moves.

Which is when I realize that I'm being **WATCHED**.

In the house next door, there's a **GIRL** with her face pressed up to the window, clearly **enjoying** my impromptu dance routine.

EEEEKKKK!

I **SCREAM** and pull the curtains shut. I throw myself onto the floor and seriously hope she is not from my new school.

Then I open up the freezer bag and pull out what looks like half the uneaten **wedding cake** wrapped in aluminium foil.

Mmm.

Icing. SO
much delicious,
sugary icing.

BEFORE

No icing left
anywhere.
I've **LICKED**
it all off.

AFTER

7:20 a.m.

REGRETTING

my life choices.

7:30 a.m.

This is my usual wake-up time. SO much has already happened
today. I take some comfort in knowing at least it **can't** get
much **WORSE.***

Time to prepare for school. I'm a little **NERVOUS**
about starting at a brand-new school mid-year. Everyone will
already be in their groups and will have found their friends.
I'm going to have to make a good **impression** to infiltrate
these tight-knit friendship circles. I need to exude **COOL!**

*SPOILER ALERT: It gets MUCH worse.

As per our Family Meeting, Dad has been placed in charge of my new SCHOOL UNIFORM. I open the wardrobe door and there, hanging neatly, are my new school clothes. Freshly ironed. Ready to wear. Khaki. ALL **KHAKI**.

(On Nan's crocheted coat hangers, of course)

ALL items of clothing have been clearly **labelled,** but Dad has been a little too **enthusiastic** with this and has stitched GIANT labels on everything. (I swear, I lose one cap—**ONCE**—in first grade and no one has ever let me forget it.)

COLOR
BY
NUMBER

1 = KHAKI
2 = KHAKI
3 = KHAKI
4 = KHAKI

VISIBLE FROM SPACE

GREAT WALL OF CHINA

GREAT BARRIER REEF

MY NAME LABELS

JUSTIN CHASE

I unroll and inspect the **socks.** They are definitely **NOT** store-bought socks. **NO** member of this family will buy socks from a shop when Nan can crochet a perfectly-good-if-not-better pair. Not on my Nan's watch. They do look particularly **soft** and **FLUFFY** and... **KHAKI.**

Complete with name labels.

I get dressed and it soon becomes evident that not only does Dad still think of me as a **Hoppy Doppys** fan, he also still thinks I wear the same size clothes as I did in **KINDERGARTEN.**

NOTHING fits me! I **struggle** to do the buttons up on my shirt. My shorts are so **tight** I can barely walk—it's more like a penguin's waddle. My jacket won't zip up.

The **ONLY** items of clothing that look like they actually belong on my body are Nan's super comfy crocheted **SOCKS**—made with **love.**

Who's the new guy?

"DAAAAAAAAAAAADDDDDDDDD!"

Dad eventually arrives. "What's wrong, Ju..." He pauses as he sees **exactly** what's wrong. My miniature school uniform!

"Mmm. Looks a **fraction** tight. But that's because it's all new. It'll stretch! By lunchtime it'll be PERFECT! Now, remember they're starting swimming classes at your school this week, so you need to pack all your swimming gear."

Of course I **remember**! When I found out there would be **SWIMMING** on my first day, I almost did a **cartwheel**. I'm not good at much, but I **CAN** swim. I've been swimming since before I could walk!

Here's my chance as the **New Kid** to impress all the other kids with my LEGENDARY swimming **SKILLS.** I had literally spent **hours** carefully considering the best swimming trunks and goggles combination to inspire awe and admiration in my classmates.

Olympic-quality, teflon-coated, advanced-grade racing trunks

Flames for added speed!

High-tech infrared, metallic, shock-absorbing goggles

I unzip my overnight bag to grab my swimming stuff. I **RUMMAGE** inside. I **gulp** and slowly rezip the bag. I take three deep breaths and unzip the bag again. Nothing has changed!

In a PANIC, I empty the contents of the bag on the ground. A pile of black clothes. **NOT** my clothes. Vlad's clothes. I've taken his bag from the car trunk by **MISTAKE!**

N00000000!

Who brings a black turtle-neck undershirt to a tropical island?!

Dad suggests I could wear his swimsuit, or as he refers to them, **the Wedgie Makers**, but it's a definite **NO**.

In total **desperation**, I even try Vlad's black, full-length, head-to-toe, UV-blocking swimsuit. Another **NO**.

"I could always write a note and you could **skip** swimming for today, Justo," Dad offers. "Your boxes will be here by tonight—I bet you've got **heaps** of other swimsuits."

"But I really don't want to miss my chance to make a first-day **splash** in the pool," I huff.

"Maybe I could be of assistance," Nan says, poking her head up the stairs, brandishing her CROCHET HOOK like **EXCALIBUR**. "I could **whip** you up a swimsuit lickety-split."

54

Somehow Nan has speed-crocheted me a pair of trunks. And they actually look pretty **decent!** A little **ITCHY**, but at this point I'm not complaining. Nan is also letting me use her **goggles** from her weekly Seniors' Aqua Aerobics class. They're prescription goggles, so they make everything look **WEIRD**, but I prefer that to chlorine in my eyes.

So crisis **AVERTED!** I am all set for my spectacular swim **STARDOM**.

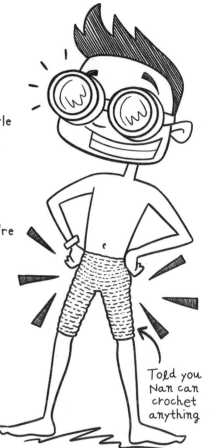

Told you Nan can crochet anything

8:45 a.m.

"I'm ready!" I announce to Dad and Nan once my new schoolbag is packed.

"You're **not** walking, Justingles! I'm going to take you! I've gotta drive you on your first day!"

I sigh **heavily**. I don't particularly want a lift to school from him because...

55

... Dad drives **THIS**. A giant **TOILET** on wheels.

THE WHIZZ WIZARD

ALL CISTERNS GO!

CALL 1-2-FLUSH

MR.P 123

Jump Justina

JUSTIN CHASE

JUSTIN CHASE

Dad's a plumber and he is **PASSIONATE** about it! He's always trying **inventive** ways to advertise his business. We spend a **LOT** of time workshopping new names together. It's kinda fun.

His latest plan involved turning his work truck into a toilet. GUARANTEED to get **ATTENTION!** Great for business. **Not so great** for your first day at a new school.

We're a block away from
the school. I'm **SLOUCHED**
down in the front passenger
seat as LOW as I can get.

"I'll just jump out here,
Dad. Thanks for the lift!"

"OK, Justapalooza. I get it. You're a **big guy** now. Don't
want to be **EMBARRASSED** by your old man. I understand.
I just need to find a spot where I can pull over."

Dad slows down to a **snail's pace.** Finding a spot big
enough to park a GIANT TOILET near a school at drop-off
time is not easy.

"Too small. Won't fit. That's a driveway. No parking.
Another driveway." Dad's running commentary of
disappointment continues as we draw **closer** and CLOSER
to the front gate of the school, meanwhile cars behind us are
starting to toot their horns in FRUSTRATION.

HONK! HONK! HONK!

CALL 1-2-FLUSH

"Here's a spot!" Dad declares **triumphantly**. The "spot" is right in **FRONT** of the school gate, where parents and students have paused to **STARE** at what's causing the CACOPHONY of car horns honking in the street.

"A bit tight, but if I reverse park, I reckon I can squeeze in, JuzzMan."

My dad can do a **LOT** of things well. Reverse parking is **NOT** one of them! As he begins slowly reversing, the automatic back-up beeper of the toilet truck starts its incessant BLARING.

Everyone on the sidewalk is now **STARING** straight at the toilet blocking the road. Hard to blame them really. Babies in strollers are **CRYING**. Kids already at school have run back to the fence, their faces poking through the rails to see what's causing all the **COMMOTION**.

I'm just a boy, sitting in a giant toilet, dying on the inside!

Finally, after a **NEVER-ENDING** succession of forward and backward maneuvers, Dad parks the truck in the space.

It feels like **every** eyeball in the suburb of Wally Valley is now focused directly on the **GIANT TOILET** on wheels in front of the school.

"Have a **great** first day, Justy!"

"Thanks, Dad." I smile **weakly**. I slowly open the door and try to **SLINK** out without drawing any more attention. Eyes down on the ground, I shuffle toward the gate.

Wishing I was invisble

Wishing I was camouflaged

Wishing I was on another planet

KA-WOOOOSSSHH!

That's Dad's customized **horn**—made to sound like a toilet **FLUSHING**—now BLASTING at a thousand decibels into the air. He leans out the truck window and shouts, "I'll pick you up here at three, Justinnitus. **LOVE YOU**, kiddo!"

"I'll **walk** home, Dad," I mouth across the sidewalk.

I turn and hurry in through the school gates and try to block out the **STARES** and MURMURS and hushed conversations, but snippets still float to my ears. Two **whispered** words are repeated over and over again.

8:57 a.m.

My eyes are down and I'm trying to **sense** my way to the front office, Jedi-style, without looking up and accidentally making eye contact with anybody. Of course, I walk straight into another kid, our chests **BUMPING** together. I look up and our eyes LOCK.

"Sorry!" I stammer.

His eyes narrow as he looks me up and down. And then he loudly says to all the kids crowded around, "Looks like **TOILET BOY** is Justin Chase's **NUMBER ONE** fan!"

What I WISH I'd replied:
"My good fellow, you have leapt to the regrettably common conclusion that I am an overly zealous fan of international recording superstar, Justin Chase—no doubt due to the fact that each item in my possession is indeed labelled with the name JUSTIN CHASE in large letters. You are, however, quite mistaken."

What I ACTUALLY reply instead:
"Ummmm."

He leans in closer. "Are you **president** of the Justin Chase **FAN CLUB,** Toilet Boy?" There are giggles in the crowd.

As **KING** of the pithy comebacks I reply, "Ummm" again.

And then he begins **singing** Justin Chase's chart-topping worldwide smash hit music single **'LET ME IN"**—with a few **VARIATIONS.**

LET ME IN

Justin Chase

LET ME IN by Justin Chase

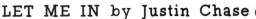

I'm locked outside your heart.
I need you to let me in.
Knock! Knock! Knock! Let me in.

Yeah, I need you to let me in,
Because the neighbors are starin'.
Knock! Knock! Knock! Let me in.

Don't make me call a locksmith,
Because they are expensive.
Knock! Knock! Knock! Let me in.

Didn't see the doorbell. Wow.
Gonna try the doorbell now.
Ring! Ring! Ring! Let me in.

I've slid a note under the door.
It's down there on the floor.
And it says: Let me in.

Terrible lyrics but SO catchy!

TOILET ME IN by Mean Kid

I'm locked outside your heart.
I need you **TOILET** me in.
Knock! Knock! Knock! **TOILET** me in.

Yeah, I need you **TOILET** me in,
Because the neighbors are starin'.
Knock! Knock! Knock! **TOILET** me in.

Don't make me call a locksmith,
Because they are expensive.
Knock! Knock! Knock! **TOILET** me in.

Didn't see the doorbell. Wow.
Gonna try the doorbell now.
Ring! Ring! Ring! **TOILET** me in.

I've slid a note under the door.
It's down there on the floor.
And it says: **TOILET** me in.

So, yeah, he just swapped in the word TOILET. To make things even worse, he has a REALLY good singing voice.

DING! DING! DING!

The bell rings and all the kids disperse, leaving me standing alone, a little in **SHOCK,** "Toilet Me In" ringing in my head. Why does it have to be so **CATCHY?** Not for the first time in my life, I **CURSE** Justin Chase! (Not me. The famous one.)

Someone rushes past me, then stops and turns around. "Hey, it's **Mr. Hoppy Doppys!** Are you starting school here?"

It's the girl that saw me dancing in my room this morning. I nod and smile while **DYING** quietly on the inside.

"I'm **Mia.**" She smiles back.

"I'm Justin." I leave out the Chase. "I'm looking for the **FRONT OFFICE.**"

"It's that big building there. At the front. With **FRONT OFFICE** in **GIANT LETTERS** on it." She points helpfully, then turns and skips off **giggling.**

I trudge up to the front office and walk in through the heavy doors.

Miss Denise picks up the microphone linked to the school's
PA system and **taps** it gently with her fingernails.

The rap-tap-tap static **ECHOES** out loudly from speakers
across the school.

"ATTENTION, STAFF.
We need a student helper from
6M to the front office to escort
JUSTIN CHASE to class."

The name crackles, **amplified**, and **hangs** in the air.

AARRGGH!

The collective HYSTERICAL, high-pitched shriek of excitement generated by classrooms full of Justin Chase fans (known by the collective term **"CHASERS"**), believing the pop star is HERE in THEIR school, **explodes** into the atmosphere. It's **DEAFENING!** And getting louder as a STAMPEDE of tween Chasers ignore their teachers' requests to:

STOP SCREAMING IMMEDIATELY!

 RETURN TO YOUR SEATS, PLEASE.

HONESTLY, SHOW SOME SELF-RESPECT!

and CHARGE to the front office, faces pressed against the glass, to catch a glimpse of their celebrity **CRUSH.**

"WAIT, WHAT?!?!"
"THAT'S NOT JUSTIN CHASE!"

I can hear the hearts breaking in bitter disappointment.

It's only Toilet Boy!

The **CHAOS** has finally died down. The Chasers have returned, disappointed, to their classrooms. And I'm STILL standing in the front office while Miss Denise smiles at me and Miss Bernice glares at me.

In through the doors **waltzes** the Mean Kid (with the lovely voice). He waves **EXCITEDLY** at me, like we're long-lost friends.

"You must be the new student! **WELCOME** to Wally Valley Public School. You're going to LOVE it here!" He beams. "I'm Marvin! I can just tell we're going to be **BEST BUDDIES!**"

What is going on?!

POSSIBLE EXPLANATIONS

Mean Kid has a twin?	Just had a lobotomy?	Can sing AND act?

"Marvin, would you be a **dear** and please escort young Justin here back to **6M** with you?" Miss Denise asks.

"It would be my **PLEASURE**, indeed DUTY, as **School Captain**, Miss Denise. I'll point out the highlights along the way too. The cafeteria. The library. The **TOILET**," he says with **emphasis**, smiling at me.

"You're a **TREASURE**, Marvin!" Miss Denise declares.

"No, you are, Miss Denise! And Miss Bernice, is that a new cardigan? It looks **EXQUISITE!**" Marvin compliments the surly front office lady. A smile crosses her face. No. Sorry. She just had something stuck in her teeth.

"Let's go, Justin. Don't want to miss any learning opportunities!" Marvin holds the door open for me.

Outside, I expect the smile to disappear and **MEAN KID** to reveal himself, but Marvin continues to be **unnervingly** charming. He leads me through the school, dutifully pointing out features, until we reach classroom **6M**.

GASP!

YOINK!

It was ME aLL aLong!

72

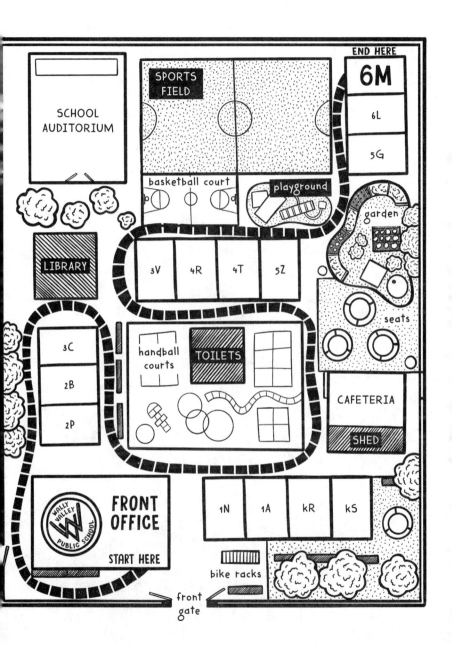

I follow Marvin through the doorway and feel every eyeball in the classroom **instantly** focus on me.

That's a LOT of eyeballs!

"**WELCOME!**" booms the teacher, standing by the martboard, as though he's SHOUTING across a canyon.

"INTRODUCE YOURSELF TO THE CLASS, NEW STUDENT!"

Ummmmm. My name is... Justin.

Chase.

A soft titter of GIGGLES escapes from the students seated in rows at their desks.

JUSTIN CHASE

"SILENCE

THERE IS <u>NO</u> GIGGLING IN MY CLASSROOM!

The class is **silent,** except for the THUD of my terrified heart **beating** against the confines of my shirt.

"WELCOME TO CLASS 6M, JUSTIN CHASE. I AM MR. MAJORS. YOU WILL ADDRESS ME AS <u>SIR</u>. SHARE THREE PERSONAL FACTS ABOUT YOURSELF WITH THE CLASS SO THAT WE CAN BOND."

"Yes, SIR! Um..." My mind goes blank.

"SHARE <u>FASTER</u>, JUSTIN CHASE!"

"Umm. I like playing VIDEO GAMES," I blurt out. There are actually some nods and smiles returned by the other kids. I notice Mia in the front row, giving me a subtle thumbs-up and a wink.

"NEXT PERSONAL FACT!"

"Umm. I'm a good swimmer," I stammer.
More encouraging smiles from the class,
except from Marvin, who is making a dramatic
display of YAWNING. That throws me.

"Umm. Umm." My mind is racing. My breath is ragged.
My heart is POUNDING again, which may explain why,
when Mr. Majors screams,

"JUSTIN CHASE! WE DO NOT HAVE ALL DAY!"

The button on my chest (which has been struggling to keep
my shirt together since this morning) can't take it anymore.

It goes FLYING across the room and hits
Mr. Majors right in the EYE! There's a mixture
of shocked gasps and nervous giggles
from the classroom.

ROAR!

Silence. Mr. Majors PLUCKS the button from his eye, his face contorted in **ANGER**.

"DETENTION!

FOR THE ENTIRE CLASS! COURTESY OF JUSTIN CHASE!

There are groans and huffs from across the classroom, all directed at ME.

"JUSTIN CHASE. TAKE YOUR SEAT, FRONT AND CENTER, AND COMMENCE LEARNING IMMEDIATELY."

He's pointing at a miniature seat and table that has been WEDGED in between the precise rows of regular desks and chairs. On one side, Marvin is smirking at me; on the other side, Mia is seated.

She whispers, "They had to get a spare desk and chair from indergarten for you. Don't worry. It's only **temporary.**"

I **CONTORT** myself into my seat, like a frog on a lily pad.

"AND NOW WE SHALL RESUME MATH MONDAY!" Mr. Majors **barks** and points toward a complicated math equation on the smartboard that may as well be **hieroglyphics.**

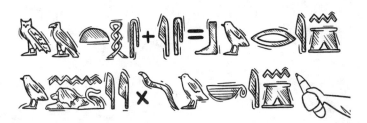

"ALL day **MATH!**" Mia leans over and whispers apologetically to me. "Except for swimming."

My heart **sinks**. Math is **NOT** my favorite subject.

MY FAVORITE THINGS AT SCHOOL (RANKED):
1. LUNCH
2. RECESS
3. SWIMMING COMPE-TITIONS
4. DISMISSAL
5. FREE TIME
6. LIBRARY
7. READING
8. COMPUTERS

38. SUBSTITUTE TEACHERS
39. ART
40. HISTORY
41. GEOGRAPHY
43. SCIENCE
44. PHYSICAL EDUCATION
45. PERSONAL DEVELOPMENT
46. CHOIR
47. MUSIC
48. DRAMA

94. TESTS
95. CLEANUP
96. SPELING
97. ASSEMBLY
98. DETENTION
.
.
.
.
99. MATH

I try to focus on Mr. Majors as he **BELLOWS** out instructions and explanations that sound more and more like a foreign language to me.

"TAKE THE REMAINDER AND DIVIDE BY THE BLAH AND THEN MULTIPLY BY BLAH TO DETERMINE BLAH..."

It's going to be a loooooooooooooong morning.

By now my **MATH MONDAY** worksheet SHOULD be looking a bit like this:

Instead it is looking a lot like this:

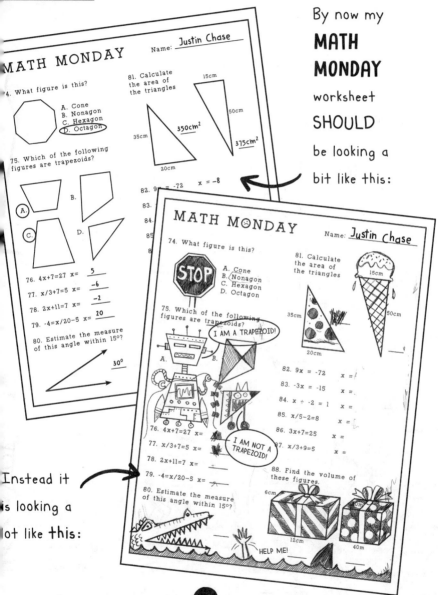

MATH MONDAY   Name: Justin Chase

74. What figure is this?

A. Cone
B. Nonagon
C. Hexagon
D. Octagon

81. Calculate the area of the triangles

15cm

50cm

35cm   350cm²

375cm²

20cm

75. Which of the following figures are trapezoids?

A.   B.

C.   D.

82. 9x = -72   x = -8

76. 4x+7=27 x= 5
77. x/3+7=5 x= -6
78. 2x+11=7 x= -2
79. -4=x/20-5 x= 20

80. Estimate the measure of this angle within 15°?

30°

MATH MONDAY   Name: Justin Chase

74. What figure is this?

STOP

A. Cone
B. Nonagon
C. Hexagon
D. Octagon

81. Calculate the area of the triangles

15cm

50cm

35cm

75. Which of the following figures are trapezoids?

I AM A TRAPEZOID!

20cm

A.   B.

82. 9x = -72   x =
83. -3x = -15   x =
84. x ÷ -2 = 1 x =
85. x/5-2=8   x =
86. 3x+7=25   x =
87. x/3+9=5   x =

76. 4x+7=27 x=

I AM NOT A TRAPEZOID!

77. x/3+7=5 x=
78. 2x+11=7 x=
79. -4=x/20-5 x=

88. Find the volume of these figures.

6cm

80. Estimate the measure of this angle within 15°?

12cm   40m

HELP ME!

81

I have to confess, I am **not** feeling well. At all. I'm starting to SWEAT and my stomach, which has been uncomfortably flittering with what I thought was butterflies all morning, is now **SWARMING** with increasingly angry killer hornets. Constant sharp, stinging jabs in my tummy are making me WINCE.

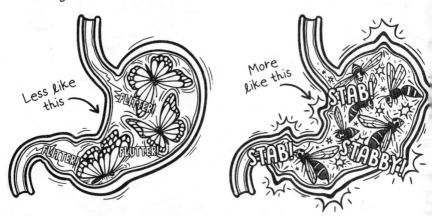

Less like this

FLITTER!
FLITTER!
FLITTER!

More like this

STAB!
STAB!
STABBY!

Something **SINISTER** is currently churning in my guts.

THE SUSPECTS

The all-you-can-eat wedding buffet

The toxic green slime smoothie

The mountain of wedding cake icing

Maybe it's the **combination** of all three? I don't know. But I do know things in my stomach are rapidly progressing to full-on nuclear **MELTDOWN.**

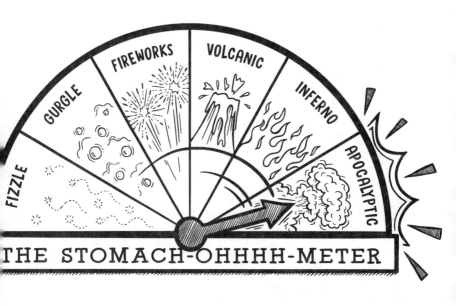

THE STOMACH-OHHHH-METER

I'm breathing **heavily** now. My stomach is **cramping** up and convulsing. My **BUTT** is CLENCHED, just in case.

One thing is certain. I NEED TO GO TO THE TOILET! **PRONTO.** And it **won't** be pretty!

Mr. Majors doesn't seem like the kind of teacher who likes interruptions, but this CAN'T wait. I timidly raise my hand into the air to get his attention.

"EXCELLENT! JUSTIN CHASE WOULD LIKE TO SHARE HIS ANSWER!"

I would **NOT** like to share my answer as I do not have an answer to whatever math question was just asked. I **WOULD** like to go to the toilet. Yet now everyone in the class is looking at me **expectantly.**

"TO THE FRONT, JUSTIN CHASE. YOU CAN SHOW US ALL YOUR WORK ON THE BOARD."

I **groan** and stand up shakily. I hover by the smartboard thinking at least I'm five steps closer to the exit. Mr. Majors holds the smartboard marker toward me like a baton.

"IMPRESS US, JUSTIN CHASE."

At this exact moment my stomach situation reaches a CRITICAL TURNING POINT and a squeaky, high-pitched **FART** escapes my **butt.** Like someone has slowly stepped on a rubber duck.

FFFSSSHHQUEEEK

My hands whip around behind me, and I push my **buttocks** together to muffle the sound. I **FREEZE** in this position, my eyes **WIDE** in:

a) shock

b) humiliation

c) fear

d) shame

e) all of the above.

Around the classroom, jaws drop in stunned **DISBELIEF.**

"I need to go to the toilet," I whisper **desperately** to Mr. Majors.

I can see my request register in Mr. Majors's head at the **EXACT** moment the smell of my errant **FART** reaches his nostrils. He recoils in **horror,** eyes watering.

"MARVIN KING, ESCORT JUSTIN CHASE TO THE BOYS' BATHROOM WITHOUT DELAY!" he orders.

"Yes, sir!" Marvin **salutes** and springs from his desk into action. "Follow me! I'll clear the way."

He **DASHES** ahead of me, out the door, and along the walkway, yelling so loudly that students and teachers in other classes stop working to peer out their windows.

"TOILET EMERGENCY!"

I follow **awkwardly** behind as fast as I dare to move while still holding on to my **BUTT,** desperately trying to avoid any more **ESCAPAGE.** Marvin has raced ahead to the bathroom and by the time I arrive, he is holding the single cubicle stall door open for me, butler-style.

"I'll leave you to it, Toilet Boy." He smirks.

I **BURST** through the toilet stall door.

Usually I wipe the seat several times and lay down an **elaborate,** protective barrier of toilet paper to ensure **no** skin comes in contact with the plastic or porcelain that has touched **A MILLION OTHER BUTTS** (thanks, Mom, for passing on your **GERMOPHOBIA** to me!)...

FLASHBACK

Toilet seats contain on average 295 bacteria per square inch!

WE'RE WAITING JUST FOR YOU, JUSTIN!

... but today there just isn't time.

I'm CLENCHING my buttocks so hard against the **DELUGE** that is coming and I know I **can't** hold it back much longer.

I **whip** my pants down in a flash and WINCE as the cold of the seat collides with my **BACKSIDE.** I open the **flood gates** and unleash the vile TORRENT of **PURE EVIL** from my behind.

It sounds like an overinflated **balloon** let go in a tiny room, RICOCHETING around the walls, expelling air in ripping, rubbery **BURSTS,** while a high-powered hose is **fired** into a metal bucket.

The smell is **HIDEOUS,** attacking my nostrils like POISONOUS gas.

My stomach clenches and **TWISTS.** I pant and **groan.** My hands are balled into fists so tight my knuckles turn white.

And then it's OVER. I feel like I've run a marathon. (Or how I imagine I would feel if I ran a marathon. I can barely make it once around the soccer field!) Mostly, though, I feel **RELIEF.** I let out a deep SIGH and reach over for the toilet paper.

The toilet roll holder is...

I turn to the other wall. **NOTHING!** I twist around in a **PANIC.** There's no spare roll on the tank. I **need** toilet paper!

Where's Nan's crocheted toilet roll dolly when you need her?

In **DESPERATION,** I look up to the ceiling. Only a few hardened, ancient spitballs. I scan the floor. Just some **MURKY** puddles of **unknown** origin.

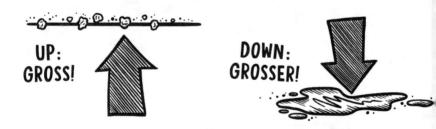

UP: GROSS!

DOWN: GROSSER!

I call out meekly, **"HELLOOOOOOOOOOOOOOOOO?"** and my voice **ECHOES** pathetically around the deserted, tiled room. I think I hear the sound of muffled **chuckling** somewhere outside in the distance.

I wait. I check EVERYWHERE a second and third time, just in case I missed an emergency stash of toilet paper hidden away somewhere. **ZILCH!** I reach down where my pants are pooled around my ankles and **rummage** through my pockets, hoping a forgotten tissue might be buried in the corners. Not even a hanky. Totally **EMPTY.**

I sit, engulfed in the PUTRID, heavy **stench.** A prisoner stuck to the toilet. I **HAVE** to wipe. I stare, defeated, looking down at my feet. That's when it hits me.

My **SOCKS!** I am going to have to SACRIFICE the brand-new, cushy, comfy socks my doting grandmother lovingly crocheted for me. And so...

SCENE DELETED

BY THE CENSORS

(IT'S FOR THE BEST REALLY)

Please enjoy these cute puppy pictures instead . . .

Apologies for the disruption to transmission.
We now resume our scheduled programming . . .

I **slink** back into the classroom, praying no one notices that I'm now missing something.

PLEEEEEASE DON'T SPOT THE DIFFERENCE!

BC
(Before Crisis)

AD
(After Desperation)

RIP socks

Mr. Majors is at his desk reading and all the students are occupied with their worksheets. I **TIPTOE** across to my desk and pull out my mini seat to sit down.

I **GASP.** There, on my chair, is a roll of **TOILET PAPER!** I react by **ramming** my chair back under the desk before anyone else sees the toilet roll.

93

Unfortunately, this sends the toilet roll **FLYING** out toward the front of the classroom. It keeps **rolling** until it **HITS** the feet of Mr. Majors, who clearly wasn't expecting to look down and see a roll of **toilet paper** balancing on his boot.

"IS THIS SOME KIND OF A JOKE?!"

His eyes follow the trail of toilet paper back to my desk, where I'm standing, mouth **AGAPE** in dismay. We're both **frozen**—me in shock, him in anger—joined together by the billowing reel of two-ply toilet paper forming a thin, white path between us.

10:45 a.m.

DING! DING! DING!

Recess! Saved by the bell **again**. Thank you, bell!! I owe you!

"CLASS IS DISMISSED FOR RECESS. JUSTIN CHASE, STAY BEHIND!" Mr. Majors BELLOWS.

There is the regular **rustle** of unzipping and shuffling as the other kids file out of the classroom. As soon as they are through the doorway, **chatter** and GIGGLES erupt.

Mr. Majors follows the path of toilet paper toward me and begins an impressive **tirade** of **SHOUTING,** which I take as my cue to mentally exit the building and travel to...

"DO I MAKE MYSELF CLEAR, JUSTIN CHASE?!"

Mr. Majors repeats, even LOUDER—if that's possible—jolting me out of my happy place and back to the classroom.

"Yes, sir!" I reply instinctively, but truthfully I haven't heard anything he's shouted.

"JUSTIN CHASE, DISMISSED FOR RECESS."

10:50 a.m.

Outside, most of the students have finished eating their snacks and are now engaged in their recess activities...

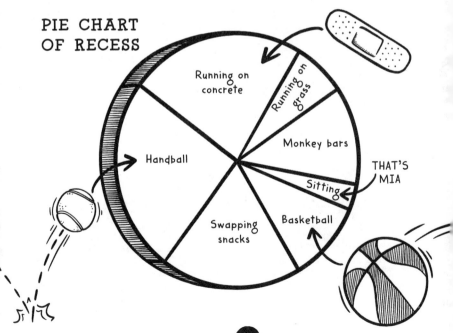

PIE CHART OF RECESS

- Running on concrete
- Running on grass
- Monkey bars
- Handball
- Sitting — THAT'S MIA
- Swapping snacks
- Basketball

I sit on the same bench as Mia, but right on the **other** end.

I peek inside the lunch box my dad packed for me. As I **FEARED**, it's all GREEN!

EAT US, JUSTIN!

GREEN IS GOOD!

NOM NOM NOM!

JUSTIN CHASE

Luckily, I'm not hungry. **At all.** I close the lid tightly and **PEEK** over at Mia. She's busy working on something in a large, GLITTERY notebook balanced on her knees.

I finally muster up the COURAGE to speak. "What are you drawing?"

Without looking up from her notebook, Mia answers, "Unicorns!"

I try not to roll my eyes. "Can I see?"

Mia stops drawing and looks across, sizing me up. After careful consideration, she decides to show me what she's working on. I immediately take back my eye roll. These unicorns are **AWESOME!**

"**WHOA!** They're so COOL!" I exclaim.

"Thanks!" Mia smiles. "I'm working on the characters for a **video game** I'm designing. It's **TOP SECRET**. Can I TRUST you?"

I nod **emphatically**. Again, Mia pauses and deliberates if I am **WORTHY** before flicking back a few pages in her notebook. She glances around the playground and shows me more concept sketches.

"I am in the presence of **GENIUS**," I declare, and Mia **GRINS** proudly and enthusiastically starts flipping through her notebook, sharing more of her drawings and ideas until...

11:15 a.m.

DING! DING! DING!

It's swimming time. MY time! I shall now completely erase the memory of **TOILET BOY** and henceforth be known as **SWIM STAR,** or something.

GOODBYE, TOILET BOY

HELLO, SWIM STAR

We grab our swimming gear and head toward the bus at the front of the school. I'm the **last** student to step on board the bus, and there is ONLY one spare seat left—at the very front. I take my seat against the window. Where **X** equals the other kids, **Y** equals the bus driver, **Z** equals friendless me, and **W** equals "Oh, please, NO! Don't sit next to me, Mr. Majors. Why, oh why, cruel world?"

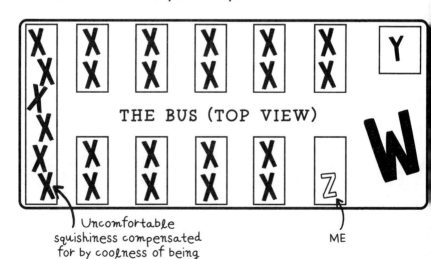

THE BUS (TOP VIEW)

Uncomfortable squishiness compensated for by coolness of being in the back row.

ME

Mr. Majors regards me with a cold **GLARE** and plonks himself on the only available seat.

BEFORE

AFTER

The bus driver peers over her shoulder, inspecting the seated passengers. When she's satisfied that everyone is in place, she gives a wink and turns to face the windshield.

"Hold on to your **UNDIES**, everyone!" She cackles, **revving** the engine like a Formula 1 race car driver in pole position.

VRRRRROOOOOOOM!

And then we're off... and RACING!

"GO TIME!"

It's like she's playing a **RACING** video game and thinks she has unlimited lives to spare. We're **ROARING** through the streets, tires screeching, plumes of smoke pouring out behind us.

Lucky for me, I'm so tightly wedged between Mr. Majors and the window, I physically can't move.

There are SHRIEKS and **SQUEALS,** and that's just Mr. Majors.

"We need some **tunes!**" the driver declares, flicking on the radio. Music **BLARES** out of the bus speakers at full volume, and I shudder as I instantly recognize the song. "Let Me In" by Justin Chase.

"I'M LOCKED OUTSIDE YOUR HEART. I NEED YOU TO LET ME IN"

Soon the entire busload of kids is singing along with the song at the top of their voices. I close my eyes and try to ignore the shouted **"TOILET"** substituted for **"to Let"** as the wild ride continues.

SCHOOL 2 POOL

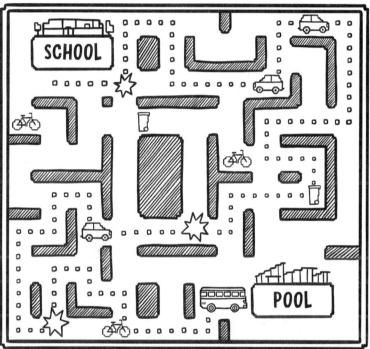

SCHOOL

POOL

PLAYER 1:

BETTY BUS DRIVER

LIVES ♥♥♡♡

STRENGTH ▮▮▮▮▮▮▮▮▯▯

REFLEXES ▮▮▮▮▯▯▯▯▯▯

TOP TIME 9:39

12 Trash Can Direct Hits

5 Stop Signs Missed

7 Cars Sideswiped

3 Bike Riders Traumatized

SCREEEEEEEEEEECH!

11:30 a.m.

We come to a JARRING halt outside the Wally Valley
Aquatic Center as the bus driver slams on the brakes and
checks her stopwatch.

My stomach is **CHURNING** again, and I take deep
breaths to calm things down. As ordered by Mr. Majors,
who isn't looking too healthy himself anymore, we file out
of the bus and proceed inside the Aquatic Center.

to the left　　　　**to the right**

Time to put on our swimsuits and goggles. It's SHOWTIME
in the pool!

All of **6M** is sitting in a row along the pool's edge, breathing in the smell of chlorine, our feet dangling in the water.

Everyone **except** Marvin. He's been excused from swimming and is still dressed in his uniform, irritatingly lounging on the seat against the wall behind us. Apparently he's doing extra work on his computer tablet—but I can tell he's actually playing games.

PEW PEW
DING DING

Mr. Majors, armed with a clipboard, is pacing behind us, shouting **extra loud** to be heard over the rabble of toddlers cavorting in the adjacent kiddie pool and the occasional huge splash of a brave diver hitting the water from the diving tower.

"TO DETERMINE YOUR INDIVIDUAL SWIMMING LEVEL COMPETENCE, EACH STUDENT SHALL DIVE INTO THE POOL AND SWIM A LAP IN THE STROKE OF THEIR CHOICE WHILE I ASSESS THEIR TECHNICAL FORM AND FINESSE. WHO WILL VOLUNTEER FIRST?"

PICK ME!
PICK ME!
PICK ME!

My hand shoots straight up. I **wiggle** my fingers and try my best puppy dog eyes. This is the moment I have been waiting for all day.

Prepare to be **AMAZED,** fellow classmates, and then get in line to be friends with the most **sensational** swimmer in the history of Wally Valley Public School!

Mr. Majors chooses someone else.

I watch on, disappointed my moment of **GLORY** has been delayed.

Oh well. My time will come soon enough! I plaster a condescending smile across my face and observe my "competition." In quotes. Ha!

They execute a flawless dive into the water, barely making a ripple, and then proceed to GLIDE through the water in an effortlessly perfect, textbook display of freestyle.

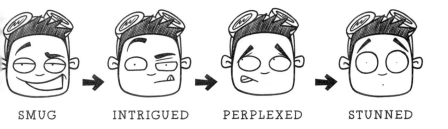

SMUG   INTRIGUED   PERPLEXED   STUNNED

"**ADEQUATE. NEXT!**" Mr. Majors yells, jotting notes on his clipboard.

ADEQUATE?! Another classmate waltzes up to the blocks and dives into the pool like an Olympic **champion**.

"**ACCEPTABLE. NEXT!**"

Student after student dives into the pool like a water sprite and **ZOOMS** to the end impressively. What is going on? I'M supposed to be the swimming legend! Swimming is MY thing!!

At my old school, I was **THE BEST**. Here, I'm AVERAGE, at best.

THEN

1st Place
SWIMMING
CHAMPION

Hereby awarded, on this momentous occasion, to:

Sir Justin Chase

and NOW

PARTICIPATION
AWARD

Justin Chase

YOU TURTLE-LY TRIED!

11:58 a.m.

Finally, I'm the only student left who hasn't been picked to swim.

"JUSTIN CHASE, YOU'RE UP!" Mr. Majors booms.

I walk to the diving blocks, rethinking my **strategy**. I decide to pull out the **BIG GUNS**. No one else has attempted butterfly stroke. Difficulty level is **HIGH,** but if I can pull it off, I might get the respect of my swimming peers. I get in position and snap my nan's prescription goggles over my eyes.

I AM BUTTERFLY MAN

VIEW WITHOUT GOGGLES

VIEW WITH GOGGLES

I'm balanced on the diving block, crouched, ready to spring into the pool. My stomach is also **CHURNING** again.

I look ahead, but unfortunately the goggles have distorted my vision and now everything seems **BLURRY.** It's now or never though. I **launch** myself into the pool and...

THWAAAAAACK!

... do the BIGGEST **BELLY FLOP** ever.

The sound **echoes** throughout the Aquatic Center, along with the gasps of sympathy from my classmates. The goggles must have messed up my depth perception and my dive was HORRIBLY misjudged. My tummy burns as the **SLAP** of the unforgiving water spreads across my delicate skin.

I try to recover, ignoring the **SHOCK** and stinging sensation radiating from my belly. I can't see where I'm going though, so I'm **ZIGZAGGING** all over the place.

To make matters worse, my crocheted trunks seem to be absorbing the water. I can feel the extra weight of the swimsuit dragging it farther down my body as I heave my way along the pool. I divert one hand to keep **yanking** it back up to my waist, leaving my other arm to continue **FLAILING** around, desperately paddling forward.

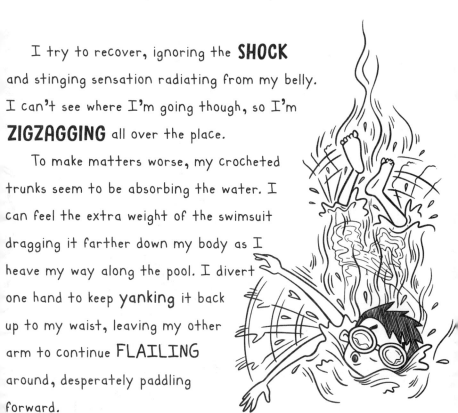

My graceful butterfly is looking more like a **DERANGED** moth missing a wing, repeatedly banging into a lightbulb.

Less like this

More like this

Eventually, no—miraculously, I touch the end of the pool. I **LURCH** out of the water looking, presumably, like some sort of angry swamp **MONSTER**. My stomach is glowing red on the outside and bubbling lava on the inside. I'm clutching my trunks, which are sagging like a potato sack, to keep them from falling off. And trying to ignore the unbearable **ITCHINESS**.

COMING TO A POOL NEAR **BEWARE**

THE BELLY FLOP BEAST

STARRING JUSTIN CHASE

I wanted to inspire **AWE**, but as I scan the faces of my new classmates, who have just witnessed my swimming debacle, I can only see...

HORROR

CONCERN

PITY

SHOCK

GLEE

Mr. Majors looks as if he's about to throw up.

To clarify, he's actually looked that way since the wild bus ride here, but he's definitely worse now. He opens his mouth to speak/shout when...

12:05 p.m. "CODE YELLOW. REPEAT, CODE YELLOW AT THE WADING POOL!"

is called out over the Aquatic Center speakers.

We all know what Code Yellow means. Some little kid has peed in the toddler pool. Our eyes move to the small, shallow splash pool. It's filled with tiny tots, and the fountain in the middle of the pool, **squirting** a spray of water over the tots, has taken on a distinct and unmistakable **YELLOW** color.

COLOR BY NUMBER
1 = YELLOW

Parents clutching their to-go coffee cups surround the wading pool and **SCREAM** as the lifeguards try to herd the **frolicking** toddlers out of the frothy, golden-tinged water.

The sight is apparently TOO MUCH for Mr. Majors and he covers his mouth and **rushes** off toward the toilets, shouting, **"MARVIN IS IN CHARGE!"** through his fingers.

I'm still desperately thinking of how to impress my classmates. And then I see the solution right there, TOWERING in front of me.

It's a brilliant combination of **DARING** and BRAVERY, sure to impress my classmates.

"I'm going to dive off the fifteen-foot platform!" I **boldy** announce to the class out of nowhere.

"YES!" enthuses Marvin. "Quick, before Mr. Majors gets back! Now, while the lifeguards are busy!" He jumps up from his seat and pushes me toward the diving platform.

12:07 p.m.

And so I find myself at the base of the diving tower ladder. My stomach is twisting in knots again, but I'm determined to show everyone how **GUTSY** I am.

I pull Nan's goggles over my eyes to obscure my vision while I'm climbing the ladder. (I'm not great with heights, so it's probably better not to be able to see exactly how high I am.) And then I begin my **ascent** to the fifteen-foot-high diving board.

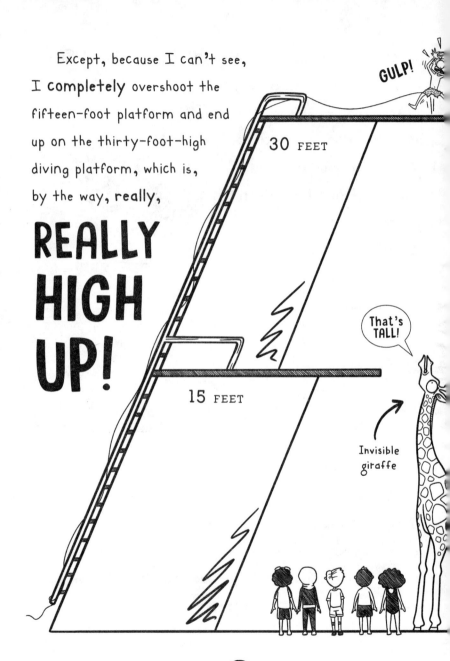

Except, because I can't see, I **completely** overshoot the fifteen-foot platform and end up on the thirty-foot-high diving platform, which is, by the way, really,

REALLY HIGH UP!

GULP!

30 FEET

That's TALL!

15 FEET

Invisible giraffe

As my brain registers how far below the pool actually is, I feel **DIZZY** and my knees go **weak**. I instinctively drop to my stomach, like a surfer paddling out to the waves, and **HUG** the diving board. I cautiously **peek** over the edge and see the upturned faces of 6M all expectantly looking at me.

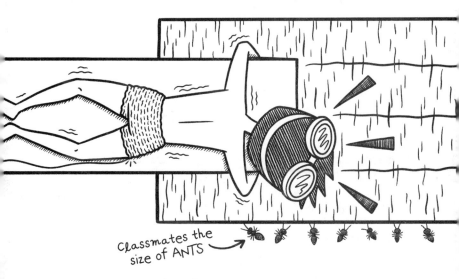

Classmates the size of ANTS

I know I need to **JUMP,** but my body is **refusing** to cooperate. I'm too **scared** to stand up, so I shimmy on my belly, like a snake, closer to the edge of the diving board. My stomach is doing gurgling **BACKFLIPS**. I had planned to do a flawless dive into the pool. Maybe even a **somersault.** Right now, I'll be **LUCKY** to even get off the diving board.

Somehow I manage to go from this...

... to this...

... to **THIS!**

And then there's a snag
in my exit strategy. Literally.
I'm **snagged** on the diving tower!
It seems a thread of yarn from my
crocheted trunks got caught on
the base of the ladder and has been
slowly unraveling.

My once thigh-length swimsuit
is now rapidly **SHRINKING!**

I'm hanging precariously from the diving board, clutching on in an increasing state of **PANIC**.

If I let go and drop down, the remains of my swim trunks will disappear. As it is now, if even a few more rows of yarn unwind from my suit, a **FULL MOON** will shine brightly above the Wally Valley Aquatic Center.

FULL MOON

UNEXPLAINED METEOROLOGICAL PHENOMENA IN LOCAL POOL

I don't want **ANYONE**, especially my new class, seeing my **BUTT!** I can't climb back up though.

NAUSEA washes over me, my stomach **CONVULSES**, and everything goes into **SLOW MOTION** right as the second wave of food poisoning strikes.

12:09 p.m.

Beads of SWEAT

SQUEEEA

Fingers SLIPPING!

"JUUUUUSSSSTIIIIIIIIIIIN CHAAAAAAAASE! GET DOWN NOOOOOOW!"

Swimsuit UNRAVELING

aka hanging by a thread

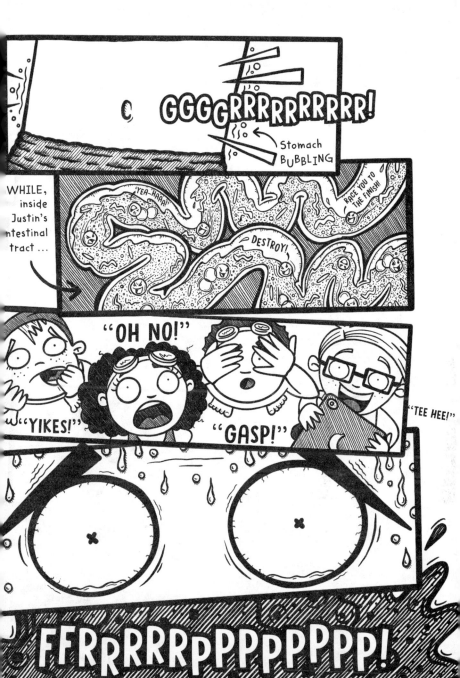

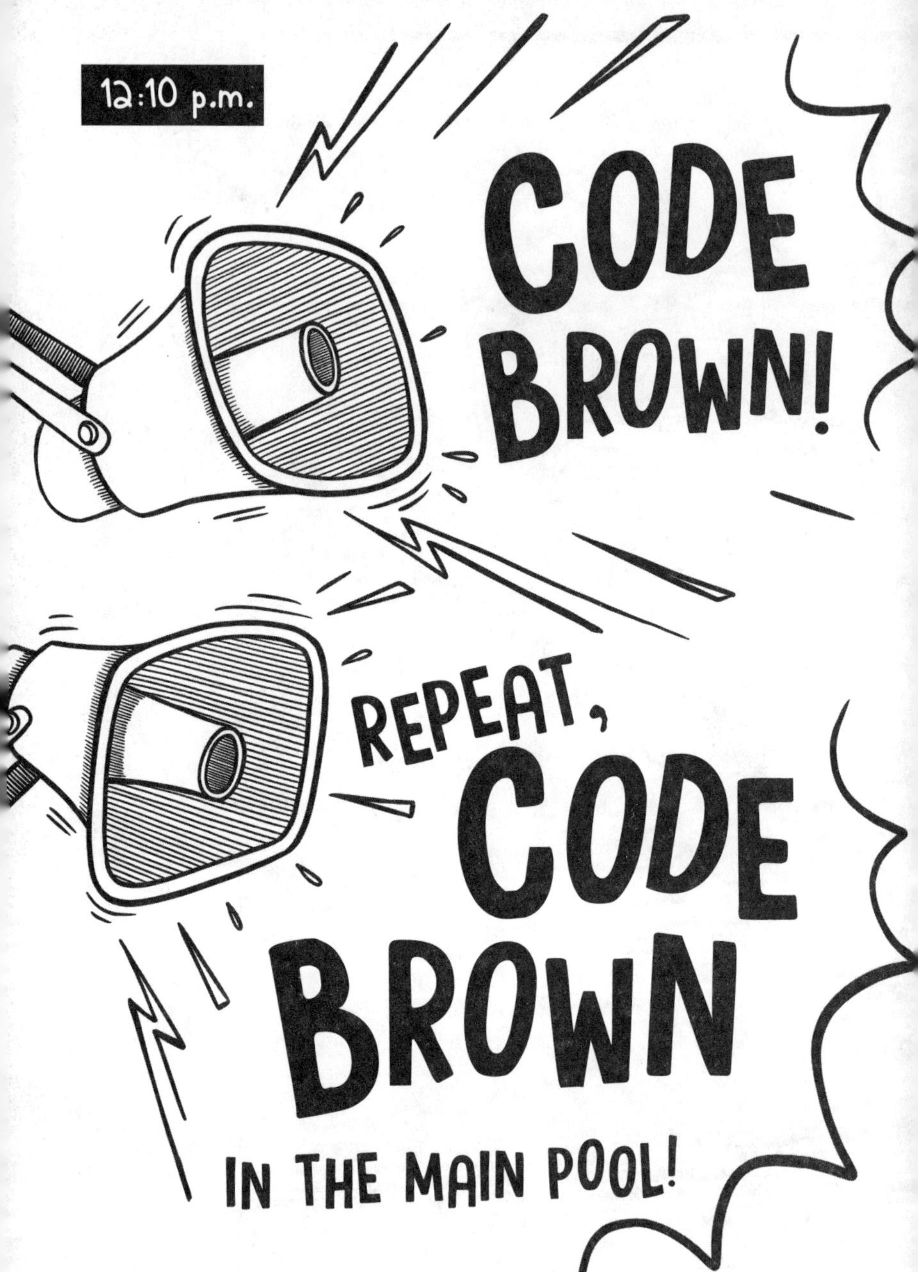
12:10 p.m.
CODE BROWN!
REPEAT, CODE BROWN IN THE MAIN POOL!

SCENE DELETED

BY THE CENSORS

(SERIOUSLY, YOU DO <u>NOT</u> WANT TO SEE THIS.)

Please enjoy these cute guinea pig pictures instead . . .

SCENE DELETED

BY THE CENSORS
(YEAH. IT'S STILL GOING!)

Please enjoy these cute quokka pictures instead . . .

SCENE DELETED

BY THE CENSORS

(UMMMMM, <u>STILL</u> GOING!!)

Please enjoy these cute baby alpaca pictures instead . . .

SCENE DELETED

BY THE CENSORS

(IT WAS THAT MESSY!)

Please enjoy these cute bunny pictures instead . . .

Apologies for the disruption to transmission.
We now resume our scheduled programming . . .

I'm the last kid back on the bus. I've been DOUSED in industrial-strength disinfectant and BLASTED with a high-powered hose. Let us NEVER speak of the details of the "pool incident" again.

I take my seat at the front, avoiding all eye contact with the other students. Mr. Majors, who has surely never SHOUTED more in his life than he has today and still looks quite ill, gives me a DEATH STARE worthy of Captain Fluffykins. He reluctantly takes his spot next to me but clearly does not want to be anywhere near me.

Now that we're all aboard, the bus driver **revs** the engine and absolutely floors it heading back to school. Perhaps she senses the change in mood of the group as she thankfully chooses not to pump the music on the return trip.

I sulkily reflect on the pool disaster. **NOTHING** went as planned. How did I get it all so **wrong?** I just wanted to fit in and impress the class and make some friends. Instead, I'll be lucky if anybody ever talks to me **EVER** again!

Not to mention how much **TROUBLE** I'm going to be in when Mom and Dad hear what happened.

I feel terrible. No, I actually feel really **TERRIBLE**. As in my stomach is **CHURNING** unbearably again. It can't be! **A third wave?!**

FFFSSSHHHQUEEEEK!

Thankfully, it's only a fart. But it is PUTRID. And it is not alone. More and more gas escapes my butt.

FFFSSSHHHQUAAACK!
FFFSSSHHHQUEEEEK!

It's like a row of rubber duckies are EXPLODING.

The **STENCH** hangs heavily in the air, and like a GHOST haunting the bus, it floats **malevolently** up and down the aisle. There are shrieks of **HORROR** and groans of DISGUST each time the smell hits a new pair of nostrils.

133

It smells worse than:

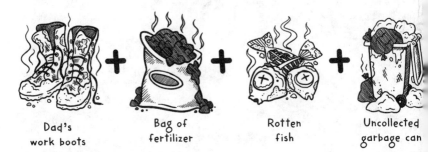

Dad's
work boots
+
Bag of
fertilizer
+
Rotten
fish
+
Uncollected
garbage can

The bus driver has caught a whiff. "HOLY MOLY! THAT STINKS!" Over her shoulder she shouts back to the passengers, "If **EVERYONE** takes a **gigantic** deep breath we can eradicate the smell. Do it for the team! One. Two. Three. **INHALE!**"

But no one is prepared to make that SACRIFICE. Hands are covering noses. Fingers are pinching nostrils shut. Shirts are being pulled up as makeshift masks. Eyes are WATERING.

The bus continues to **CAREEN** wildly down the road at full speed, everyone on board imprisoned with my **pungent** gas. Mr. Majors has now turned as green as my lunch box.

"OK, passengers! Crack open the windows, then! We need some fresh air!" the driver orders.

The fresh air hasn't helped Mr. Majors though. His flushed cheeks are PUFFING in and out. **Sweat** beads on his exceptionally large forehead. His eyes WIDEN, and then he somehow shout-whispers, **"I'M GOING TO BE SICK!"**

Uh . . . oh.

Mr. Majors **lunges** over me and thrusts his head out the window. He heaves violently and releases an impressive outpouring of **VOMIT** into the world. The speed of the bus and the flow of the air sends the SPRAY hurtling backward where it would have **SPLATTERED** all over the other windows—IF they were closed.

Unfortunately, the windows are all OPEN.

A shower of **BARF** rains back into the bus. It isn't good.

There are SCREAMS. Then there is more **BARF**.

A **chain reaction** begins.

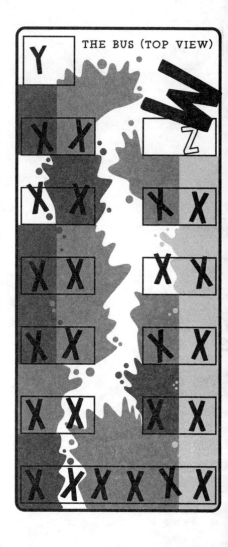

THE BUS (TOP VIEW)

KEY

ZONE 1

Those unlucky souls by the window, flecked in Mr. Majors's barf, are the first to blow chunks.

ZONE 2

This triggers a spate of secondary sympathy spewers, releasing their own vomit.

ZONE 3
Which in turn sets in motion a torrent of tertiary upchuckers, unable to ignore the sound of retching.

W = Mr. Majors
X = Students
Y = Bus Driver
Z = Me

Only a few ironclad stomachs survive the **PUKEATHON**.

If anything at all remained in my GUTS, I'm sure it would be coming out now too.

Puddles of sick are sloshing around the floor of the bus as it motors on. The smell is **putrid,** the sight HORRENDOUS.

"Emergency pit stop!" yells the bus driver as she makes a hard left that sends **RIPPLES** through the layer of **vomit** sliding around on the bus floor.

"Keep the windows open and hold your breath!" she commands as she drives us and the bus straight into the...

WALLY VALLEY WONDER CAR WASH

1 SP33D

We are **SQUIRTED** and hosed.

SOAPED and **sudsed.**

SCRUBBED and buffed.

FANNED and **blow-dried.**

And then the driver takes us through again for a **second** time.

As we drive out of the car wash, we are all positively **SPARKLING**. Any trace of the puke reaction has been polished away—but **not** the memory. No, the memory shall **HAUNT** us all for a long, long time.

FLASH FORWARD

30 YEARS IN THE FUTURE

AAARRRGGGHHH! VOMIT! EVERYWHERE!!

There, there, Mr. Majors. It was just a bad dream!

The bus driver puts the pedal to the metal and soon we're **SCREECHING** down the road to school. We can't pull up right at the front though. There's a fire engine parked at the gate. And an emergency service vehicle. And... **A GIANT TOILET ON WHEELS!** As we file out of the bus and walk to the gate, my mind is **racing**.

Mr. Majors leads us via the side pathway to the auditorium. As we skirt around the edges of the school, we catch **glimpses** of what has happened.

The handball courts look like a swimming **POOL,** with school equipment **bobbing** up and down like inflatable toys. The **EMERGENCY** crew is piling sandbags around the classrooms to hold back the rising water level. The smell is **TERRIBLE!**

And in the middle of it all
is the BATHROOM.
A **GEYSER** of water
is spraying up out
of the roof. Water is
gushing from the windows.
An unspeakable, bubbling
CAULDRON of MUCK
swirls around the school.

The procession of 6M students stops **dead** in their tracks.

Their screams of fear ECHO around the school as out of the MURKY sludge a terrifying **CREATURE** emerges.

As the **creature** slowly turns around toward the SCREAMS, the true **HORROR** is revealed. It's DAD! Waving and smiling at me!

"Just doing some **exploratory** work. Now I'm heading into the **MOUTH** of the **BEAST**," he shouts, pointing toward the overflowing bathroom. "Wish me luck, son!"

I drop my eyes to the ground and keep walking, pretending I don't hear my dad and that I don't hear the whispers of the other kids.

IS THAT TOILET BOY'S DAD?

THAT'S TOILET BOY'S DAD?

LIKE FATHER, LIKE SON!

TOILET MAN AND TOILET BOY!

1:27 p.m.

As a class, 6M marches into the dusty auditorium, where the other classes of the school are already all sitting, cross-legged, on the floor. On the stage at the front, a lady with a microphone stops talking and stares over at us with one eyebrow raised.

"I'll just **wait** until 6M is settled."

"That's the principal." Mia leans over and whispers to me, "Ms. King."

"WAITING." Ms. King **TAPS** her foot.

"STILL waiting." The eyebrow goes higher.

"Just **WAITING** a little LONGER it seems." Her eyelids blink dramatically.

"Good. **Finally**. Now that we're all here, we can continue," Ms. King trills.

TAP
TAP
TAP

"While we wait patiently for an update, I shall take the opportunity to remind you that tomorrow is school photo day. **FULL** school uniform! It is also the SUPER SCIENCE SPECTACULAR, which will, no doubt, be thrilling."

1:30 p.m.

DING! DING! DING!

"**Ignore** the bell," Ms. King chimes. "That bell would usually be marking the end of the period, but today is **exceptional.** Our Monday has **NOT** quite gone to plan."

"You can say that again, sister!" I think. Except I didn't think it. I **said** it. Out loud. LOUDLY.

BEFORE

AFTER

Ms. King's raised eyebrow is now so high it appears to be floating above her head. **"Who** spoke?" she asks with a chilly glare.

I **FREEZE,** hopeful that if I don't move, the attention will soon pass. I'm staying perfectly still. Not blinking. Not breathing. I am an inanimate object. A **STATUE** who definitely did **NOT** just blurt **"You can say that again, sister!"** to my new school principal during an assembly.

I plan to remain this way FOREVER, except out of the corner of my eye I see Marvin pointing at me manically, like he's poking holes in the air.

NOTHING TO SEE HERE.

I reluctantly raise my hand slowly toward the ceiling.

"Stand up!" Ms. King commands.

149

I cautiously rise to my feet, jutting out among the sea of heads of the other students, all cross-legged on the floor. Every kid has twisted around to see who the **NUISANCE** is. Every teacher seated along the side is glaring at the TROUBLEMAKER.

GULP

"And who do we have here?" Ms. King inquires.

"J–J–Justin Ch–Ch–Chase," I stammer. And the whole hall giggles.

TEE HEE HEE HEE HEE!

There is a moment of **bewilderment,** and then Ms. King's expression suddenly softens. "Our new student! Well, how **lovely.** Everyone please join me in welcoming Justin Chase to Wally Valley Public School."

"**WELCOME, JUSTIN CHASE,**" the entire school of children drone in unison, stretching out each syllable in a moaning chant. And it **doesn't** sound very welcoming at all.

I REALLY want everyone to stop looking at me and I **REALLY** want to sit down. But as I go to sit, I'm suddenly not sure if I'm allowed to sit down and so I stand back up again. And then, in my **nervousness,** I repeat the same action. Over and over.

Like I'm a piece of toast popping up and down

Or a YO-YO

I'm still bobbing up and down uncertainly as the rear doors of the auditorium are flung open with a **BANG**. Everyone gasps in surprise. Thankfully everybody stops looking at me and stares at the silhouette LOOMING in the doorway.

Unfortunately, that silhouette is my **dad**.

He **strides** into the hall. He's covered in **GRIME** and leaves a trail of water behind him as he heads toward the stage. In one hand he holds a bucket, in the other hand he is wielding a **PLUNGER** like he's the Statue of Liberty. (Or Statue of **Lavatories.** Might be a good business name. I should write that down.)

"Make way! Coming through! Oh, hey, Justo Chusto." I'm still **frozen** in mid-squat. He waves enthusiastically with the plunger, **flicking** some **unknown** liquid around the auditorium. There are shrieks of **HORROR.**

THIS ISN'T HAPPENING. THIS ISN'T HAPPENING. THIS ISN'T HAPPENING.

"Make way! Coming through!" he continues until he's reached the stage, where the principal appears to be momentarily lost for words. Her eyes are wide as she gazes at Dad like she's **hypnotized.**

Ms. King snaps out of her **TRANCE** and makes a flowery gesture with her arm toward Dad. "Boys and girls, our brave plumbing **HERO,** Mr. Chase. **Justin's father.**"

I groan inside.

Dad turns and faces the assembly. "Everyone can **RELAX!** The **crisis** has been AVERTED. The flooding has stopped. And, most importantly, the **CULPRIT** responsible has been DISCOVERED!" He nods toward the bucket in his hands.

"Oh my!" Ms. King warbles, fluttering her eyelids.

"But first, I would like to take this opportunity to talk to you about my **PASSION**: **TOILETS**. We all need them. We all use them. But sometimes we don't treat toilets with the **respect**, care, and **LOVE** that they deserve!"

The patch over Dad's heart!

Dad is gaining energy with his monologue. Ms. King seems to be **fanning** herself as she inches closer. "Sometimes we flush things down the toilet that we shouldn't. And that's **bad**. Very **BAD**. I've been in the sewers and I've seen things—**TERRIBLE** things! Some things do not belong in a toilet. Don't be in a rush to flush! Repeat after me: Don't be in a rush to flush!"

"**DON'T BE IN A RUSH TO FLUSH**," we all, slightly perplexed, **CHANT** in unison.

"Otherwise, something like **THIS** could happen!" And with a **flourish,** Dad jams the plunger into the bucket, then dramatically **THRUSTS** the plunger high up into the air like a triumphant gladiator. Ms. King actually swoons.

Lodged in the cup of the plunger is a **gruesome** clump of furry **MUCK.**

ICK!

EEWWW!

GROSS!

YUCK!

Cries of disgust from the students **AND** teachers fill the hall.

I don't make a sound though. My heart has stopped beating. I recognize that **foul, FETID** ball of festering **FRIZZ**. And I know that once that tangled, sodden mass of gunk is unraveled, the horrible, **SHOCKING** truth will be revealed—complete with the name labels.

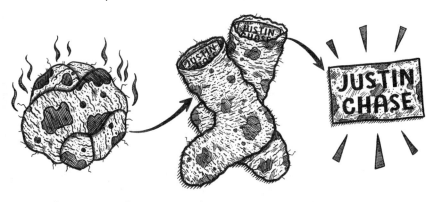

It's my socks! It wouldn't take Sherlock Holmes to solve

It was Justin Chase, in the bathroom, with a pair of fluffy socks.

this mystery.

I am so **BUSTED!**

The **shame.**

The **HUMILIATION.**

My dad will be

HEARTBROKEN.

He'll probably

disown me!

My life is **OVER!**

Dad lowers the plunger and I resign myself to my **fate**.
Soon my unfortunate **FLUSHING** indiscretion will be exposed
to the entire school. But just as my dad is about to inspect
the woeful wad more closely, a **MIRACLE** happens.

NICKERS leaps into the air and snatches the FUNKY
chunk of coiled-up socks in her jaws and **bounds** off the stage.
She scampers through the **SCREAMING** crowd and disappears
out the door, taking the evidence with her.

"NICKERS!" yells Dad furiously.

He stomps off the stage and through the parted sea of children, following in the dog's wake. His repeated cries of **"NICKERS"** continue to float in through the open doors but gradually fade away to nothing. Ms. King runs off after them. CHAOS erupts in the auditorium as the teachers on the sidelines try to settle the rowdy **rabble** of kids.

I take this as my cue to finally sit down among all the **COMMOTION.** I sigh the heaviest SIGH of relief ever sighed in the history of heavy sighs. Did Nickers and her thieving tendencies just **save the day?**

Nickers, you're my hero!

SUPER DOGGO

"That was **WILD!**" Mia whispers to me, a smile spread across her face.

"That was..."—I pause—"**something,**" I concede.

And we both giggle.

2:00 p.m.

We're back in the classroom now, eating our very late lunch at our desks, as the playground is still being **pumped** clean of the last remains of flood water. There is silence, except for the sounds:

CRUNCH! MUNCH! SLURP! SIP!

Not me though! My stomach feels fully recovered, but there's **NO WAY** I'm touching what's in my lunch box.

Mr. Majors is at his desk, his head resting facedown on the table. I don't think **HE** has recovered from the events of the day. He has **no more SHOUTS** left to give at this stage. We are under strict instructions to eat lunch and then complete **ALL** the Math Monday worksheets. Anything unfinished has to be done as homework.

DO NO
DISTUR

"JUSTIN CHASE AND MARVIN KING REPORT TO THE PRINCIPAL'S OFFICE IMMEDIATELY," crackles the school's speakers.

Mr. Majors doesn't even look up from his desk. He just extends his arm and points at the door, flicking his finger.

Marvin and I have taken a seat outside the principal's office. As directed by Miss Bernice, we are not touching anything or **chitchatting** or engaging in any form of **TOMFOOLERY**.

The **side-eye** action is off the charts though!

And my panic levels are **SOARING**. I am about to get into TROUBLE. For **something**. I'm just not sure exactly what at this stage.

161

Different **scenarios** are running through my mind.

I **glance** across at Marvin. If I'm going down, I'm pretty sure I can take him down with me! I bet his **FINGERPRINTS** are all over that missing roll of toilet paper. If there had been some toilet paper, none of this would have happened, so he's definitely **GUILTY** of something.

I'm wondering **where** exactly that roll of toilet paper is—last seen on the floor of 6M on page 95—when the door to the principal's office **flings** open.

We've been expecting you.

Come in, please, boys.

We step inside her office.

PRINCIPAL KING

BANG! The door slams shut behind us and both Marvin and I **JUMP** into the air.

I'm taken aback to see my father standing there behind us, **BLOCKING** the doorway.

"Hello, Juzzy Chuzzy," he says in a grave kind of way that scares me a little.

"Um, hi, Dad," I **splutter.**

"Sit down, please, boys," Ms. King instructs, pointing to the chairs in front of her desk.

"Yes, Ms.," I reply.

"Yes, Mom," Marvin says.

I smirk that he's accidentally called the principal **"Mom."** That's the kind of thing that typically happens to **me.** But then pieces suddenly **CLICK** in my brain and the framed portrait of Marvin and Ms. King on the desk confirms everything.

I **GROAN** on the inside. There's no way Marvin is going to get any of the **BLAME** for anything now! He's the principal's **SON.**

Dad slowly walks around the office until he's next to Ms. King. They look at each other and he nods **solemnly.**

Ms. King turns her gaze back to us.

"Now, boys, there is something very **SERIOUS** that we need to discuss with you both."

I brace myself for the **WORST.** They discovered the socks. They know I **FLOODED** the school. I need to pay the cleaning costs of the **CODE BROWN** incident at the Aquatic Center. The bus driver is pressing charges against Mr. Majors, who in turn is pressing charges against me. All my Math Monday answers are **wrong.** There are so many possibilities, but I'm **NOT** expecting to hear Ms. King say this: "When Mr. Chase came to the school to enroll Justin a few months back, well, we, as they say, hit it off. And, um, yes, we're now...

DATING!"

The blood drips are my addition for dramatic effect.

I really wish I had a **GIGANTIC** glass of water right now so I could take a massive **swig** and then **SPIT** it all out again in **SHOCK!**

SPLOOSH!

Dad has put his hand on the principal's shoulder, and she is, in turn, **patting** his hand affectionately. They look lovingly at each other as though there might be a harp playing **ROMANTIC** music in the background and **LOVE HEARTS** floating through the air.

PRINCIPAL KING

The side-eye has turned to **wide**-eye. **Neither** Marvin nor I can believe what we've heard or what we're seeing.

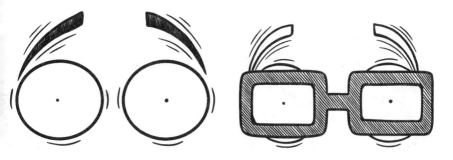

"Exciting news, eh, Just Chops?" Dad **BEAMS**. "And I'm looking forward to getting to know you, Marvy. I've heard so many great things about you! Your mom's a very special person. I'm sure we're **ALL** going to be spending a **LOT** of time together in the future!"

So... my dad is **dating** my new PRINCIPAL, who is the mother of my **ARCHNEMESIS**.

I'm walking back to class, **shell-shocked**. Marvin's a few steps in front of me right now. I'm doing my best laser eyes into the back of his head. As if he can feel it, he stops and faces me, **blocking** my path. He's smiling, but it's less of a "let's put everything behind us and be friends" smile and more of an "**EVIL**, deranged clown set on **REVENGE**" kind of smile.

Less like this   More like this

"That was some really big news," he says. Then the smile **vanishes** from his face. "Now I have some even bigger news for you. So listen up, **Toilet Boy.** For however long my mother and your dad are together as a couple" —and we both **SHUDDER** at this point—"I will devote **EVERY** waking minute of my life to ensuring that yours is **MISERABLE**."

Marvin's smile returns, he spins around, and skips back into the classroom. I trail behind. Mr. Majors is still facedown on the desk and everyone else is **toiling** away on their Math Monday worksheets. I slump onto my mini chair and **STARE** as the clock on the wall slowly **tick, tick, tick, ticks,** until, finally, MERCIFULLY, thankfully, it's...

3:00 p.m.

DING! DING! DING!

DISMISSAL!

I trudge behind the rest of the class as they **rush** for the school gate. I'm relieved to see there's no toilet truck parked anywhere on the street. No sign of Marvin either.

I look straight ahead to avoid any eye contact, which is probably why I **TRIP** over a **BUMP** in the path, landing right on my knee.

169

"Wow. It really isn't your day, is it?"

I look up, and Mia is standing there with her hand outstretched to help me up.

"Worst Monday **EVER!**" I concede.

"Since we're neighbors, wanna walk home together?" Mia asks.

I nod happily and we stroll side by side. Mia does all the talking, telling me more **TOP SECRET** info about her unicorn game, and by the time we reach our houses, I **almost** feel human again.

3:10 p.m.

"See you tomorrow, Justin Chase!" Mia waves. I wave back and walk up to our front door, where I'm immediately **KNOCKED** over by Nickers.

WHO'S A GOOD GIRL?

WHERE'D YOU GO, NICKERS?

WHERE ARE THE SOCKS?

WOOF*

WOOF**

WOOF***

*Me! I'm a good girl.
**I ran straight home.
***They're buried in the backyard with the rest of my treasure. Your shameful secret is safe with me, small human.

I say hi to Nan, who is busy drinking tea, crocheting, and yelling at a stranger on the radio.

Then I check Captain Fluffykins's food bowl. It's untouched. It's **NEVER** untouched!

I search the **entire** house, looking for any trace of Captain Fluffykins. No sign of my cat anywhere. I continue the search outside and I'm still looking in the front yard when Dad pulls into the driveway.

"Hey, Justy Wusty!" He's lumbering out of the truck. "Little bit of **EXCITEMENT** today with all that **flooding** business! And glad you got to meet Marjorie. I mean, Ms. King! Wait, you've called your mom, right?"

My heart stops. I **haven't** called Mom. I totally **FORGOT**. This isn't good. I promised I would call as soon as I got home. I **DASH** inside and rummage through my schoolbag, looking for my phone, which has been on silent all day.

MOM

49 Missed Calls

Monday 10:35 a.m.

Justin!

Monday 10:36 a.m.

JUSTIN!!

Monday 10:37 a.m.

JUSTIN CHASE!!!

Monday 10:38 a.m.

You've got some explaining to do, Mister!

Monday 10:39 a.m.

HOW did you manage to take Vlad's bag??!?!?!?

Monday 11:21 a.m.

Kinda funny!

You're still in trouble!

Monday 11:47 a.m.

Call me as soon as you get home.

Monday 11:51 a.m.

The pool here is amazing! How did swimming go?! What did you do about your trunks?! 🤿

Monday 12:10 p.m.

Hope your day is going great! 🖐️ 😊 💜

Monday 12:27 p.m.

So much food! I hope your dad isn't giving you TOO much junk food. Try to at least eat something green!

Monday 12:29 p.m.

Brush your teeth

And floss!

Monday 12:31 p.m.

Call me as soon as you get home.

Monday 12:45 p.m.

MISS YOU!!!

Monday 12:50 p.m.

Hope your day is going great! 😊 👍 💜

Monday 1:15 p.m.

Look how big the hotel bathroom is! There's a whole pyramid of TP! We'll never run out 😜

Monday 1:35 p.m.

Your eyes are closed in nearly every single photo!

Monday 1:37 p.m.

EVERY photo!!!

Monday 1:38 p.m.

You're still very handsome!

Monday 2:05 p.m.

Don't forget to feed Captain Fluffykins!

Monday 2:30 p.m.

WATCH THIS!! 😺 🤣

Monday 3:00 p.m.

Hope you had a great first day at school!

I can't wait to hear all about it!

Call me as soon as you get home.

Monday 3:10 p.m.

Are you home yet?

Why haven't you called!

PICK UP THE PHONE!

Monday 3:15 p.m.

Do your homework!

Call me first

4:00 p.m.

I run up to my room and **call** Mom, giving her a **GROVELING** apology and a VERY selective account of my first day.

THINGS I MENTION	THINGS I DON'T MENTION
Mr. Majors (Mom: "A strict teacher is good!")	Socks TP Code Brown
Math Monday (Mom: "Math is very important!")	The Diving Tower The Bus Ride of Horror
Super Swimmers (Mom: "Competition is healthy!")	Captain Fluffykins Marvin Dad and Ms. King

No reason to ruin her honeymoon with all the **DISASTEROUS** details!

Her questions about my day have now transitioned to instructions and I just repeat my mantra of **"Yes, Mom"** over and over again. Suddenly a parcel flies in through the window, **HITTING** me right in the head.

THWACK!

I open the package. It's a Wally Valley school uniform and a note.

I walk over to the window and there's Mia, standing at her window, waving at me with a goofy smile.

"And have you made good friends, Justin?" Mom asks.

"Yes, I've made A good friend," I answer, waving back at Mia.

4:25 p.m.

Homework. Homework. Homework. Homework. Homework. Homework. Math Monday just **NEVER** ends! I **STRUGGLE** through the worksheets, trying desperately to get them all done. My **brain** can't take much more.

6:00 p.m.

"DINNER, JU CHU!" The call floats up from below. I am **SO** ready to eat again. I bound down the stairs into the kitchen.

"What are we eating?" I ask hopefully.

"Steak and chips!" Dad grins.

Finally, some **REAL** food! Except when my plate is placed on the table, I realize we are still suffering under the brutal **Green Diet** dictatorship.

"Cabbage steak and kale chips." Dad beams.

Nan rolls her eyes.

"Think I'll make a pot of tea."

ALL GREEN!

I'm in my room. I should be unpacking now, except my boxes, filled with **EVERYTHING** I own and cherish, have been declared **"temporarily misplaced"** by the company that was meant to deliver them all to Dad's house this afternoon.

Captain Fluffykins is also still **"temporarily misplaced."** We've searched everywhere **AGAIN,** inside and out. I'm getting really worried.

NOTHING has gone right today.

MISSING!

CAPTAIN FLUFFYKINS

MISSING!

MY WORLDLY POSSESSIONS

MISSING!

MY HOPES AND DREAMS OF FITTING IN

I'm lying in bed, EXHAUSTED. Who knew constant **indignity** was so tiring? I'm just so relieved that the day is nearly over. I slowly drift off to sleep, ranking my Monday **FIASCOS** from bad to **WORST.**

11:55 p.m.

PPSspSPSspPSPszZZZzPZpzPZZPz

A sudden **whining**, high-pitched **BUZZING** sound jolts me awake. I sit up in my bed, disorientated. My room is cloaked in **DARKNESS**, except for a strange fluorescent blue **LIGHT** emanating from the stairwell.

Wake U CRoppy Doppy

I reach over and **flick** the switch of my lamp, but it doesn't turn on.

PPSspSPSspPSPszZZZzPZpzPZZPz

The **NOISE** is more **intense** now. I slink out of bed and wrap my blanket around me like a CAPE. I hit the light switch for my room, but again, nothing. Just darkness, except for the **GHOSTLY** glow from below.

PPSsPSPSsPPSPsZZZZZPZ

I **tiptoe** cautiously down the stairs to the second story of the house. I can hear my dad **SNORING**, and my nan **SNORING** even more thunderously, in their respective rooms.

"Dad!" I **squeak** softly at his doorway. "Dad!" There's no answer. He is a heavy sleeper though, so it's not too surprising.

THINGS DAD HAS SLEPT THROUGH

New Year's Eve fireworks

The smoke alarm

Next door's ALL night party

And there's no point calling for **Nan**. Her hearing aids would be out now. Along with her teeth. And her glasses. And her hair. She's basically just a **shriveled** ball of **WRINKLY** skin in a nightgown at the moment.

The noise is getting louder and **LOUDER.** I wish Mom was here. Her **bravery** would be coming in handy right about now.

THINGS MY MOM ISN'T AFRAID OF

The Dark   Monsters   Ghosts

Since she's not here, I think about what she would do **IF** she was. And I know she would **march** right down the stairs and discover that Dad has left the television on again (**"TYPICAL!"**) and turn it off and then give me one of her snuggly **HUGS** and then go straight back to sleep.

So I do exactly what Mom would do.

I march **BOLDLY** down the stairs. (OK, so maybe I **SLIP** down the steps, but the blanket is really bulky and heavy and keeps getting caught under my feet.)

THUD

THUD

I head into the living room and **indeed** find that the television is on.

STATIC is flickering across the screen, illuminating the room in an eerie, luminous blue. The whiny **BUZZ** emitting from the television has reached an ear-piercing pitch.

PPSPZPZZPSZ!

I pick up the remote control and click the power button OFF... but nothing happens. I try to turn the volume down, but the sound continues **ROARING**.

I yank the power cord out of the socket and yet the TV is still **FIZZING** with light and babbling scratchy noise.

I stare, **dumbfounded**, at the television as the static clears and an image slowly comes into focus on the screen.

It can't be?

It might be!

It is!
CAPTAIN FLUFFYKINS!

At which point I faint and everything goes black...

And if you thought MONDAY was bad,

just wait until...

Things are about to really blow up!

The next WORST WEEK EVER installment
COMING SOON!

WORST WEEK EVER

MONDAY	TUESDAY

WEDNESDAY	THURSDAY	FRIDAY

SATURDAY	SUNDAY

FUN FACTS

WITH JUSTIN CHASE

Don't be too afraid of toilet seats and germs! There are typically **TEN TIMES** more GERMS on a **cell phone** than a toilet seat! **YIKES!**

One hundred years ago most **swimsuits WERE** actually knitted from WOOL, so Nan's idea of **crocheting** a pair of trunks isn't TOO weird.

EXCALIBUR is the name of the legendary SWORD of King Arthur. In the famous story, Merlin the Magician puts the sword in a stone and only the **true king** can pull it out again.

Flushing anything other than poo, pee, or toilet paper **IS** very **BAD**. There are now giant, rocklike lumps of flushed nonbiodegradable matter, congealed fat, and household waste clogging up sewer systems around the world. They're called **FATBERGS!!**

Kale CHIPS are **NOT** chips, despite what anyone tells you!

DRACULA, the vampire from Bram Stoker's novel (first published in 1897), is the most filmed literary monster ever. He's been in hundreds of movies!

There are over **700** hieroglyphic symbols in the **Ancient Egyptian** alphabet. Imagine how hard their spelling tests would be! They didn't need to learn **punctuation** though, because they didn't use any!

HOW TO DRAW:
JUSTIN CHASE

STEP 1
Start with two ovals for eyes.

STEP 2
Draw the face around the eyes—kinda like a square with round corners.

STEP 3
Do dots for the pupils and a little curved line for the nose.

STEP 4
Draw the eyebrows and mouth next—these features determine his expression.

STEP 5
Add in the hair, with a zigzag line across the top.

STEP 6
Then draw the ears— "C" shapes on both sides of the head.

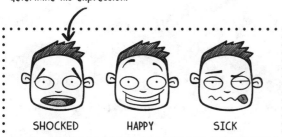

SHOCKED   HAPPY   SICK

STEP 7
For the finishing touch, color in his hair and mouth.

WHAT'S <u>YOUR</u> PREDICTION FOR

TUESDAY?

_____

_____

_____

_____

_____

_____

_____

Draw an illustration of Tuesday.

AND NOW...A BRIEF MESSAGE FROM

EVA & MATT

SHE WROTE THE WORDS

HE WROTE THE OTHER WORDS **AND** DREW THE PICTURES

BABY EVA:
All about the accessories, even at an early age.

BABY MATT:
Used to be kinda cute. What happened?!

Hey there _____,

YOUR NAME HERE   (Unless this is a library book. In that case, just imagine your name here. Or use invisible ink.)

Firstly, can we just say that YOU are definitely our most favorite reader ever and are incredibly talented AND very good-looking. Secondly, THANK YOU so much for choosing to read our silly book.*

We hope that, just maybe, it made you:

a) smile

b) giggle

c) snort chortle

d) throw up in your mouth a little bit

e) all of the above.

*Assuming you have actually read it and didn't just skip through to this page, but we'll give you the benefit of the doubt.

EVA AMORES is an author and designer/photographer who has worked f[...] the Sydney Opera House and the Australian Broadcasting Company. She was born in the Philippines and moved to Australia during high school. She likes shoes, traveling, and more shoes.

MATT COSGROVE is the bestselling author/illustrator of the Macca the Alpaca series and the Epic Fail Tales series. He was born and raised in Western Sydney. He likes chocolate, avoiding social interactions, and more chocolate.

Eva and Matt met when they were randomly placed together for a group assignment at university twenty-five years ago and they've been collaborating ever since. They've made dinner, cakes, a mess, the bed, mistakes, memories, poor fashion decisions, and two actual humans, but this is their first book together.

When they were in lockdown and the world felt a bit grim, they could have mastered sourdough or binge-watched Netflix but, no, they decided to create this series instead—**WORST WEEK EVER!** (Sorry about that.)

Here are photos of Eva and Matt so if you ever see them in real life you know to run in the opposite direction.

We had heaps of fun dreaming up the ludicrous situations in WORST WEEK EVER. The events are mostly fictitious (thankfully!), but some were inspired by things that really happened to us. Like when Eva started at a brand-new school (but in another country!) mid-year, complete with a school uniform incident. Or when Matt had an epic, never-ending food poisoning experience (on an overnight train and ferry trip from Spain to Morocco—warning: Do NOT order the black squid ink paella!).

It's good to have a laugh about it. (Now. Not at the time!)

Anyway, we hope you NEVER have a week like Justin! See you Tuesday.

Best wishes,

Eva ♡ Matt ☺

P.S. If you've had diarrhea (hard to spell, worse to smell!), we DON'T recommend going to your local swimming pool and hanging off the thirty-foot-high diving tower in a crocheted suit. In real life, that's really bad and not very clever. In a book, that's perfectly acceptable and highly entertaining!

P.P.S. Keep reading! The best way to try out lots of books is to be a member of your local library. Can you believe there are FREE books just waiting for you to borrow them? OK, so you do have to return them, but then you can borrow MORE free books! How amazing are libraries?! Answer: REALLY amazing!

P.P.P.S. Don't be in a rush to flush!!